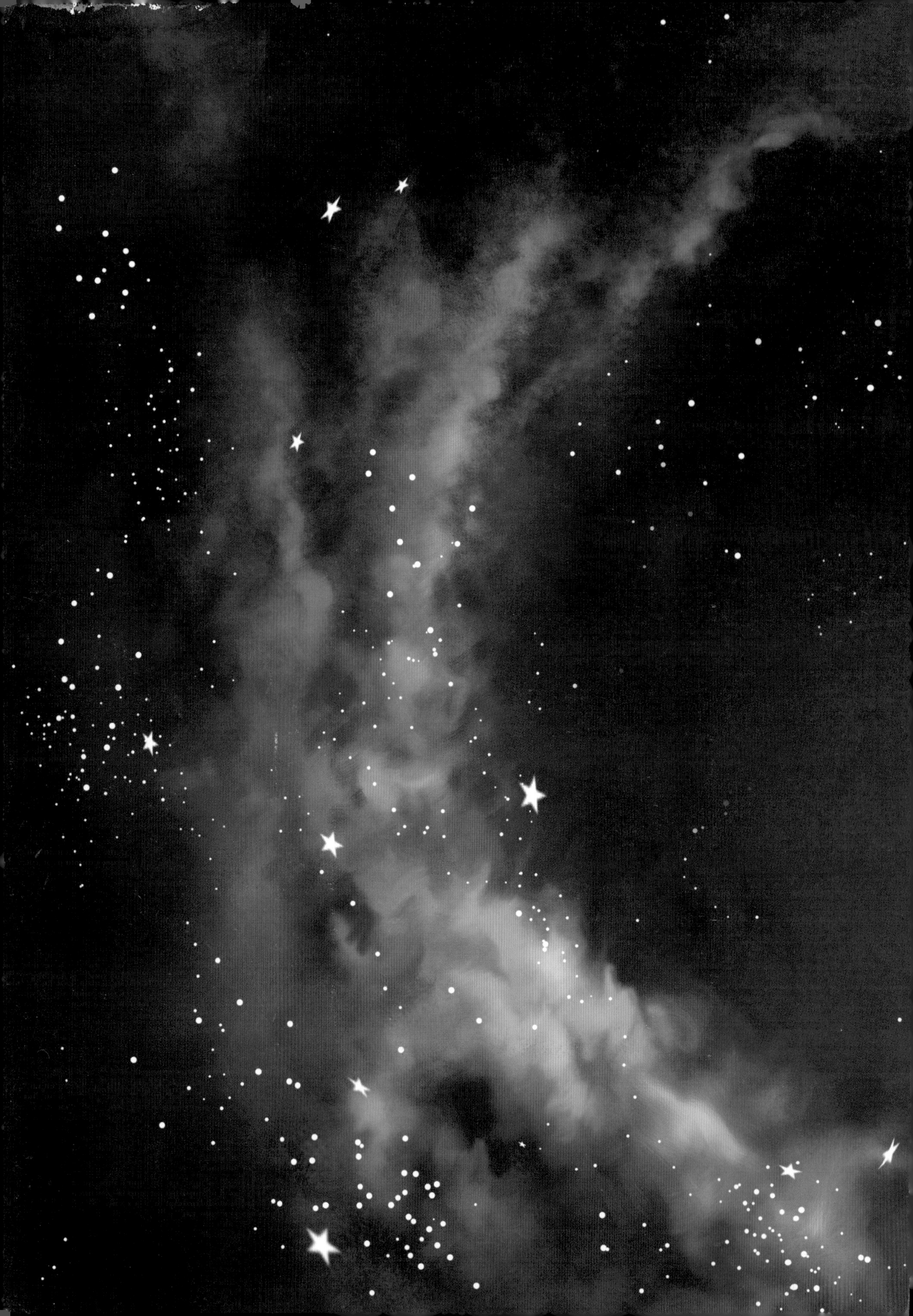

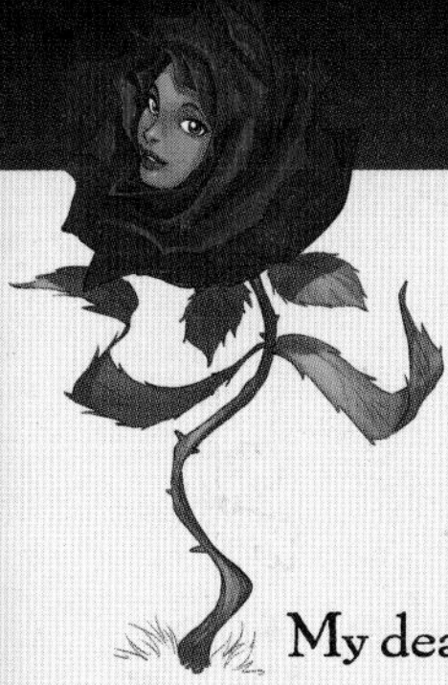

My dear Rose,

It's been only a few days since we left, but my heart is heavy at the thought of being so far from you. And it seems that this voyage has only just begun.

Good news: we've finally picked up the path of the Snake by following the trail of vanishing planets. Fox and I have decided to visit all the worlds that are about to disappear into darkness, to intervene before the Snake can inject his venom there. The first planet that we've found is a hostile land, scoured by violent winds. Is this the work of the Snake?

Knowing that you're reading these words fills me with courage. Don't worry. All will be well...

The Little Prince

First American edition published in 2012 by Graphic Universe™.

Le Petit Prince ™

based on the masterpiece by Antoine de Saint-Exupéry

© 2012 LPPM
An animated series based on the novel *Le Petit Prince* by Antoine de Saint-Exupéry
Developed for television by Matthieu Delaporte, Alexandre de la Patellière, and Bertrand Gatignol
Directed by Pierre-Alain Chartier

© 2012 ÉDITIONS GLÉNAT
Copyright © 2012 by Lerner Publishing Group, Inc., for the current edition

Graphic Universe™ is a trademark of Lerner Publishing Group, Inc.

Graphic Universe™
A division of Lerner Publishing Group, Inc.
241 First Avenue North
Minneapolis, MN 55401 U.S.A.

Website address: www.lernerbooks.com

Library of Congress Cataloging-in-Publication Data

Dorison, Guillaume.
  [Planète des Éoliens. English]
  The Planet of Wind / by Delphine Dubos ; adapted by Guillaume Dorison ; based on the masterpiece by Antoine de Saint-Exupéry ; illustrated by Élyum Studio, Diane Fayolle, and Jérôme Benoit ; translation, Carol Klio Burrell. — 1st American ed.
    p. cm. — (The little prince ; #01)
    ISBN 978–0–7613–8751–0 (lib. bdg. : alk. paper)
    1. Graphic novels. I. Fayolle, Diane. II. Benoit, Jérôme. III. Saint-Exupéry, Antoine de, 1900—1944. Petit Prince. IV. Élyum Studio. V. Petit Prince (Television program) VI. Title.
PZ7.7.D67Pl 2012
741.5'944—dc23   2011047352

Manufactured in the United States of America
1 — DP — 7/15/12

THE NEW ADVENTURES
BASED ON THE MASTERPIECE BY ANTOINE DE SAINT-EXUPÉRY

The Little Prince

THE PLANET OF WIND

Based on the animated series and an original story by Delphine Dubos

Design: Élyum Studio
Adaptation: Guillaume Dorison
Artistic Direction: Didier Poli
Art: Diane Fayolle
Backgrounds: Jérôme Benoit
Coloring: Digikore
Editing: Didier Poli
Editorial Consultant: Didier Convard

Translation: Carol Burrell
Bonus Story Translation: Anne and Owen Smith

Graphic Universe™ • Minneapolis • New York

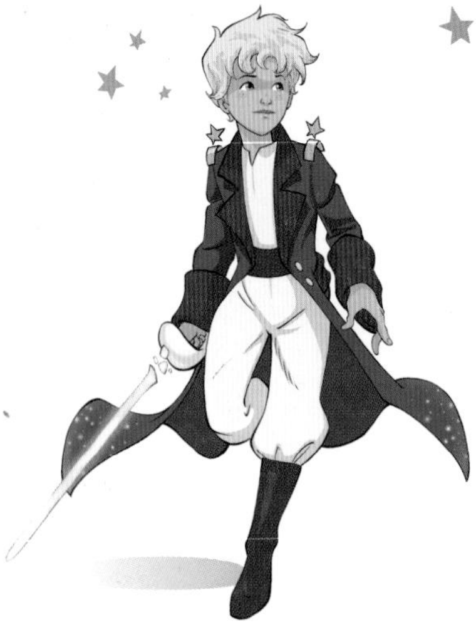

THE LITTLE PRINCE

The Little Prince has extraordinary gifts. His sense of wonder allows him to discover what no one else can see. The Little Prince can communicate with all the beings in the universe, even the animals and plants. His powers grow over the course of his adventures.

The Prince's uniform:
When he wears the uniform of a prince, he is more agile and quick. When faced with difficult situations, the Little Prince also carries a sword that lets him sketch and bring to life anything from his imagination.

His sketchbook:
When he is not in his Prince's clothing, the Little Prince carries a sketchbook. When he blows on the pages, they take wing and form objects that he'll find very useful. Like his sword, it's powered by stardust collected on his travels.

FOX

A grouch, a trickster, and, so he says, interested only in his next meal, Fox is in reality the Little Prince's best friend. As such, he is always there to give him help, but also just as much to help him to grow and to learn about the world.

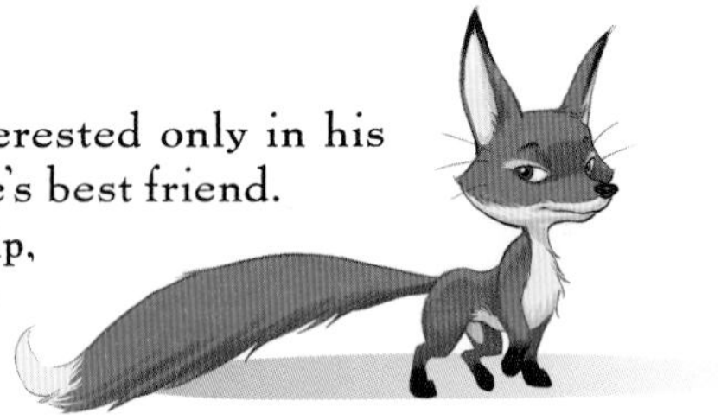

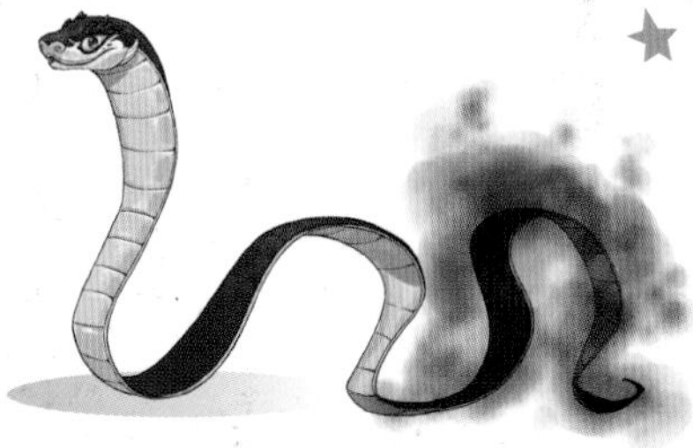

THE SNAKE

Even though the Little Prince still does not know exactly why, there can be no doubt that the Snake has set his mind to plunging the entire universe into darkness! And to accomplish his goal, this malicious being is ready to use any form of deception. However, the Snake never takes action himself. He prefers to bring out the wickedness in those beings he has chosen to bite, tempting them to put their own worlds in danger.

THE GLOOMIES

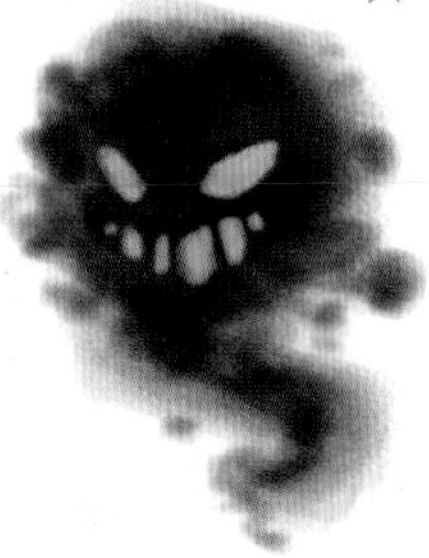

When people who have been "bitten" by the Snake have completely destroyed their own planets, they become Gloomies, slaves to their Snake master. The Gloomies act as a group and carry out the Snake's most vile orders so as to get the better of the Little Prince!

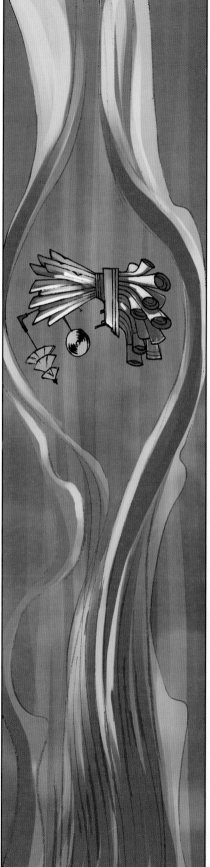

FATHER, THE WINDS ARE TOO STRONG. WE HAVE TO GO BACK!

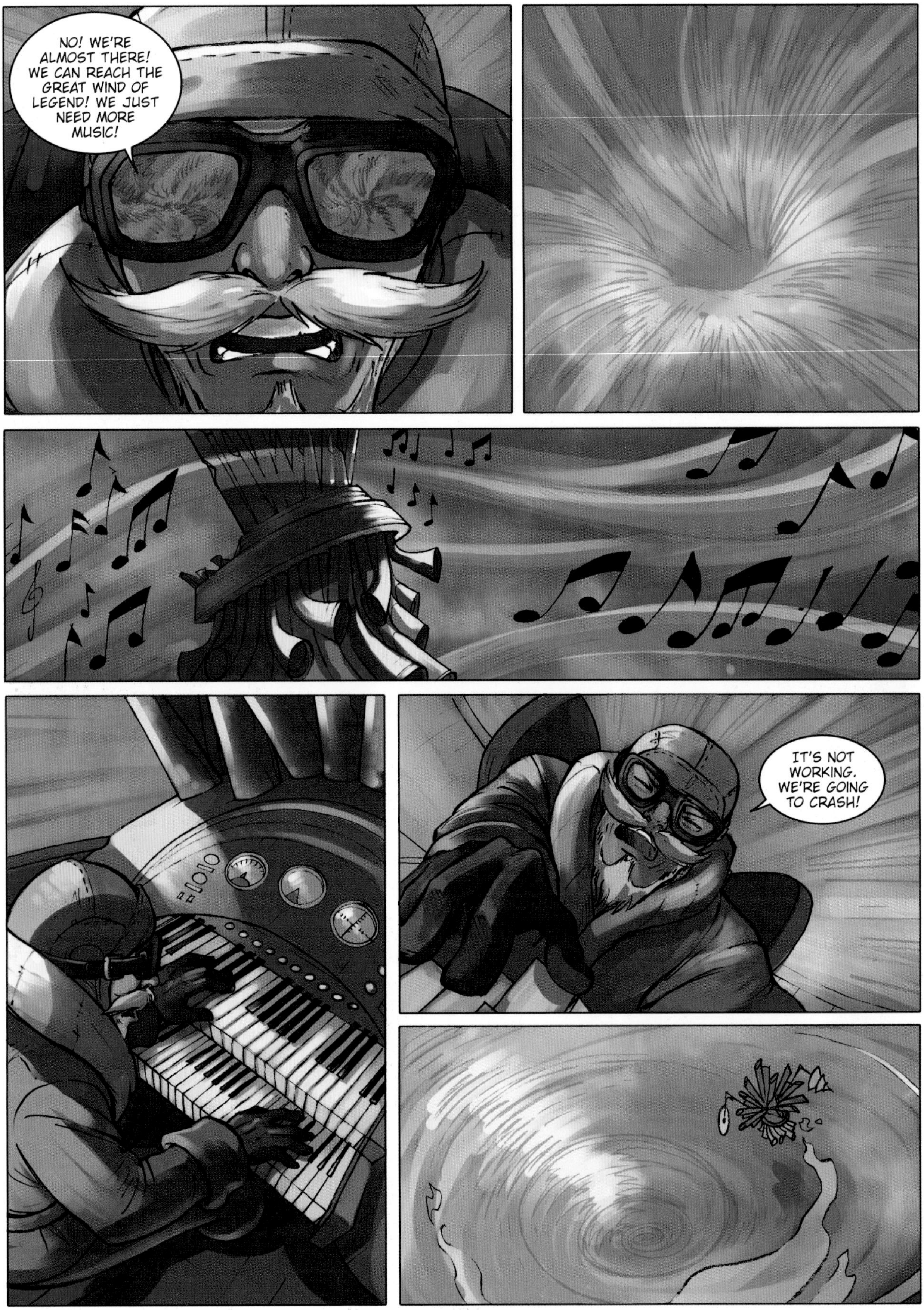
NO! WE'RE ALMOST THERE! WE CAN REACH THE GREAT WIND OF LEGEND! WE JUST NEED MORE MUSIC!
IT'S NOT WORKING. WE'RE GOING TO CRASH!

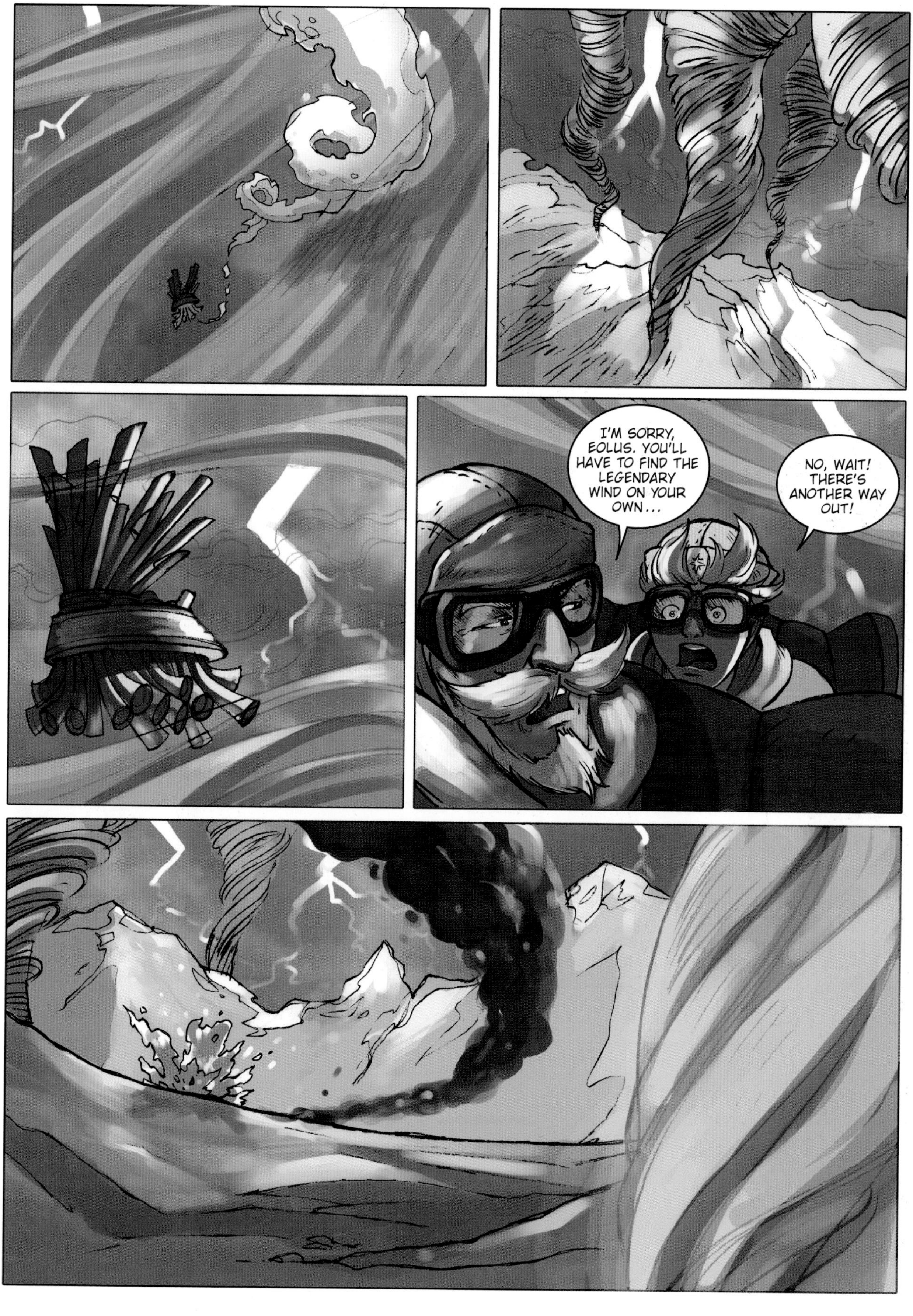
I'M SORRY, EOLUS. YOU'LL HAVE TO FIND THE LEGENDARY WIND ON YOUR OWN...
NO, WAIT! THERE'S ANOTHER WAY OUT!

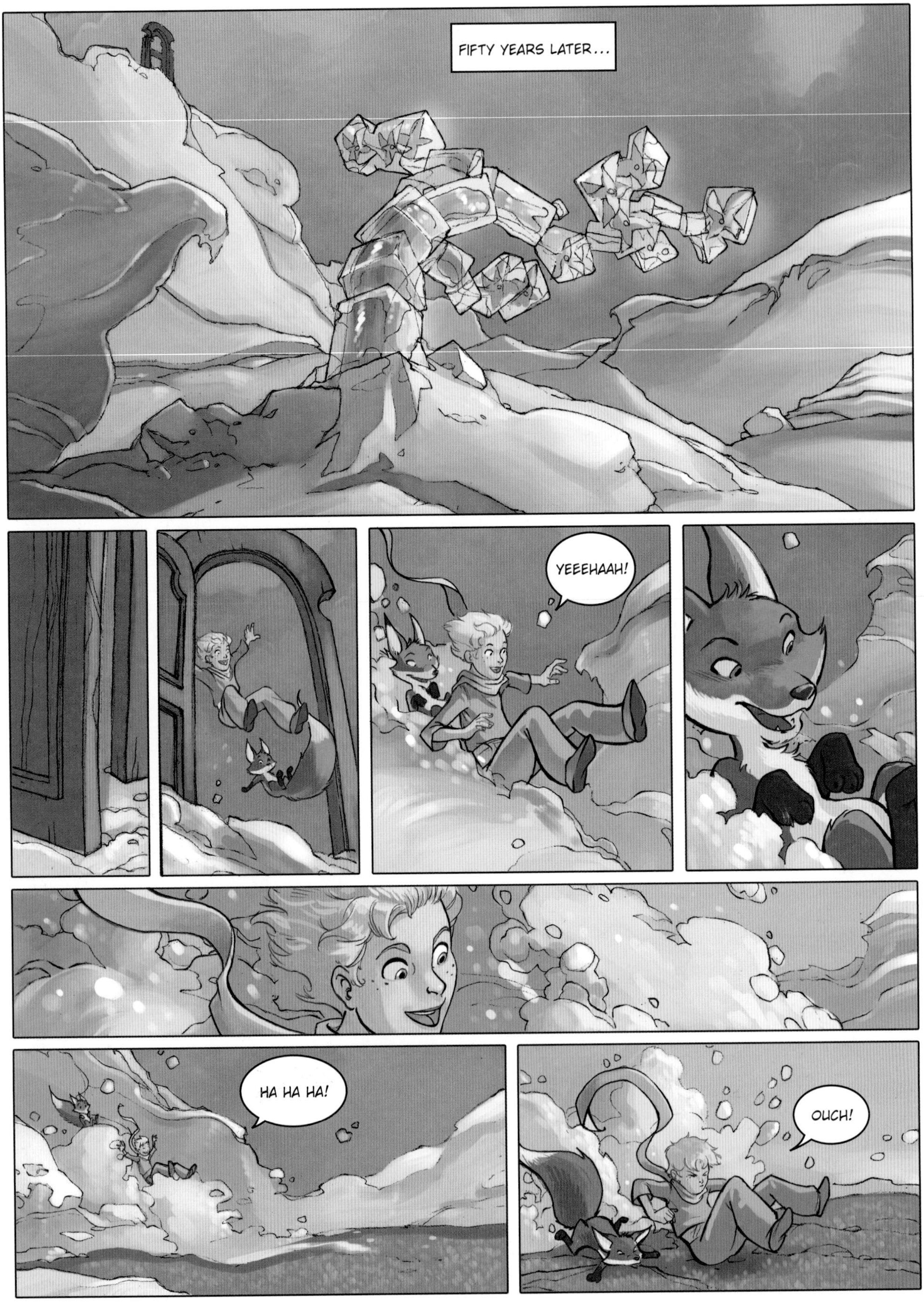
FIFTY YEARS LATER...
YEEEHAAH!
HA HA HA!
OUCH!

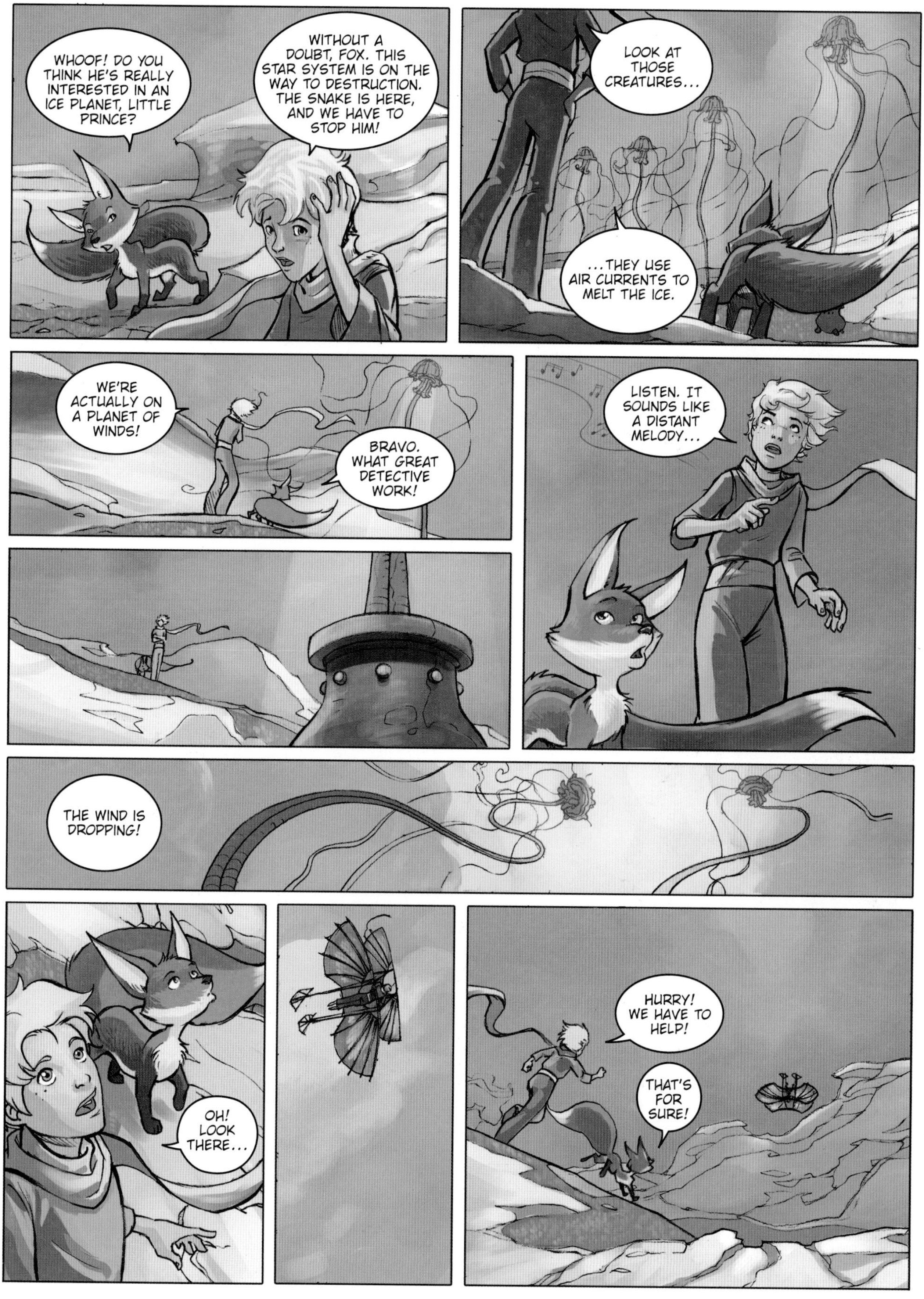
WHOOF! DO YOU THINK HE'S REALLY INTERESTED IN AN ICE PLANET, LITTLE PRINCE?
WITHOUT A DOUBT, FOX. THIS STAR SYSTEM IS ON THE WAY TO DESTRUCTION. THE SNAKE IS HERE, AND WE HAVE TO STOP HIM!
LOOK AT THOSE CREATURES...
...THEY USE AIR CURRENTS TO MELT THE ICE.
WE'RE ACTUALLY ON A PLANET OF WINDS!
BRAVO. WHAT GREAT DETECTIVE WORK!
LISTEN. IT SOUNDS LIKE A DISTANT MELODY...
THE WIND IS DROPPING!
OH! LOOK THERE...
HURRY! WE HAVE TO HELP!
THAT'S FOR SURE!

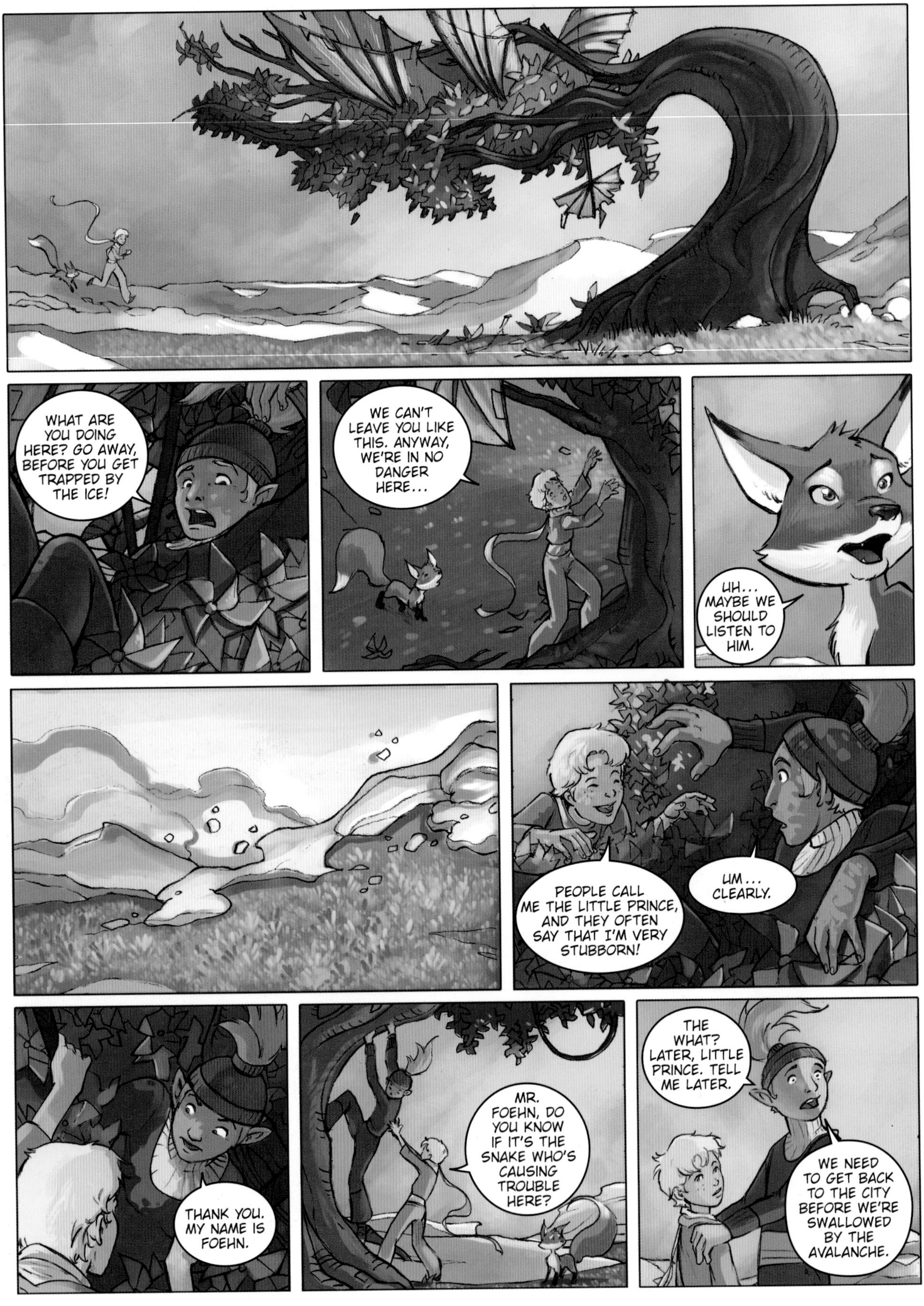
WHAT ARE YOU DOING HERE? GO AWAY, BEFORE YOU GET TRAPPED BY THE ICE!
WE CAN'T LEAVE YOU LIKE THIS. ANYWAY, WE'RE IN NO DANGER HERE...
UH... MAYBE WE SHOULD LISTEN TO HIM.
PEOPLE CALL ME THE LITTLE PRINCE, AND THEY OFTEN SAY THAT I'M VERY STUBBORN!
UM... CLEARLY.
THANK YOU. MY NAME IS FOEHN.
MR. FOEHN, DO YOU KNOW IF IT'S THE SNAKE WHO'S CAUSING TROUBLE HERE?
THE WHAT? LATER, LITTLE PRINCE. TELL ME LATER.
WE NEED TO GET BACK TO THE CITY BEFORE WE'RE SWALLOWED BY THE AVALANCHE.

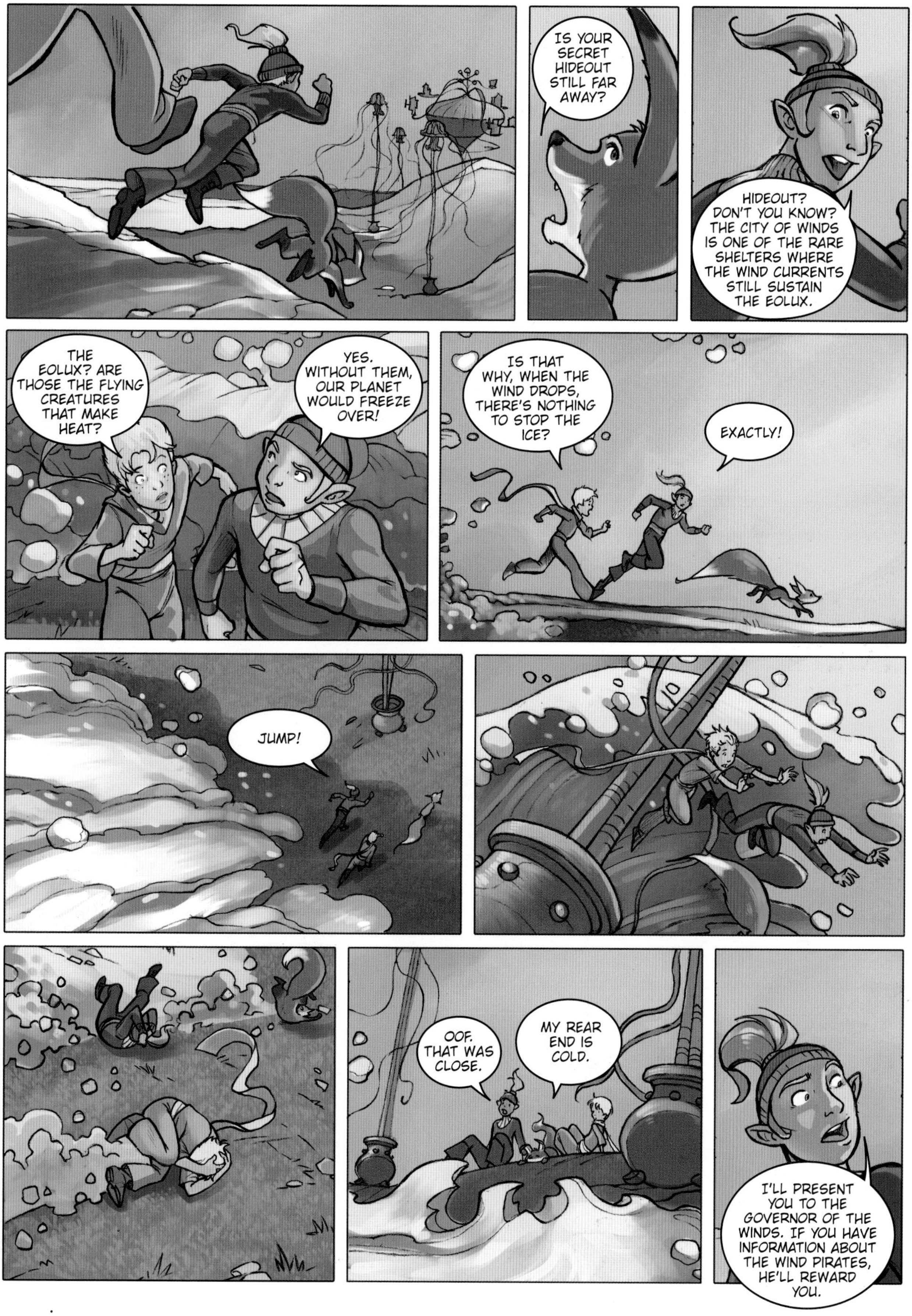
IS YOUR SECRET HIDEOUT STILL FAR AWAY?
HIDEOUT? DON'T YOU KNOW? THE CITY OF WINDS IS ONE OF THE RARE SHELTERS WHERE THE WIND CURRENTS STILL SUSTAIN THE EOLUX.
THE EOLUX? ARE THOSE THE FLYING CREATURES THAT MAKE HEAT?
YES. WITHOUT THEM, OUR PLANET WOULD FREEZE OVER!
IS THAT WHY, WHEN THE WIND DROPS, THERE'S NOTHING TO STOP THE ICE?
EXACTLY!
JUMP!
OOF. THAT WAS CLOSE.
MY REAR END IS COLD.
I'LL PRESENT YOU TO THE GOVERNOR OF THE WINDS. IF YOU HAVE INFORMATION ABOUT THE WIND PIRATES, HE'LL REWARD YOU.

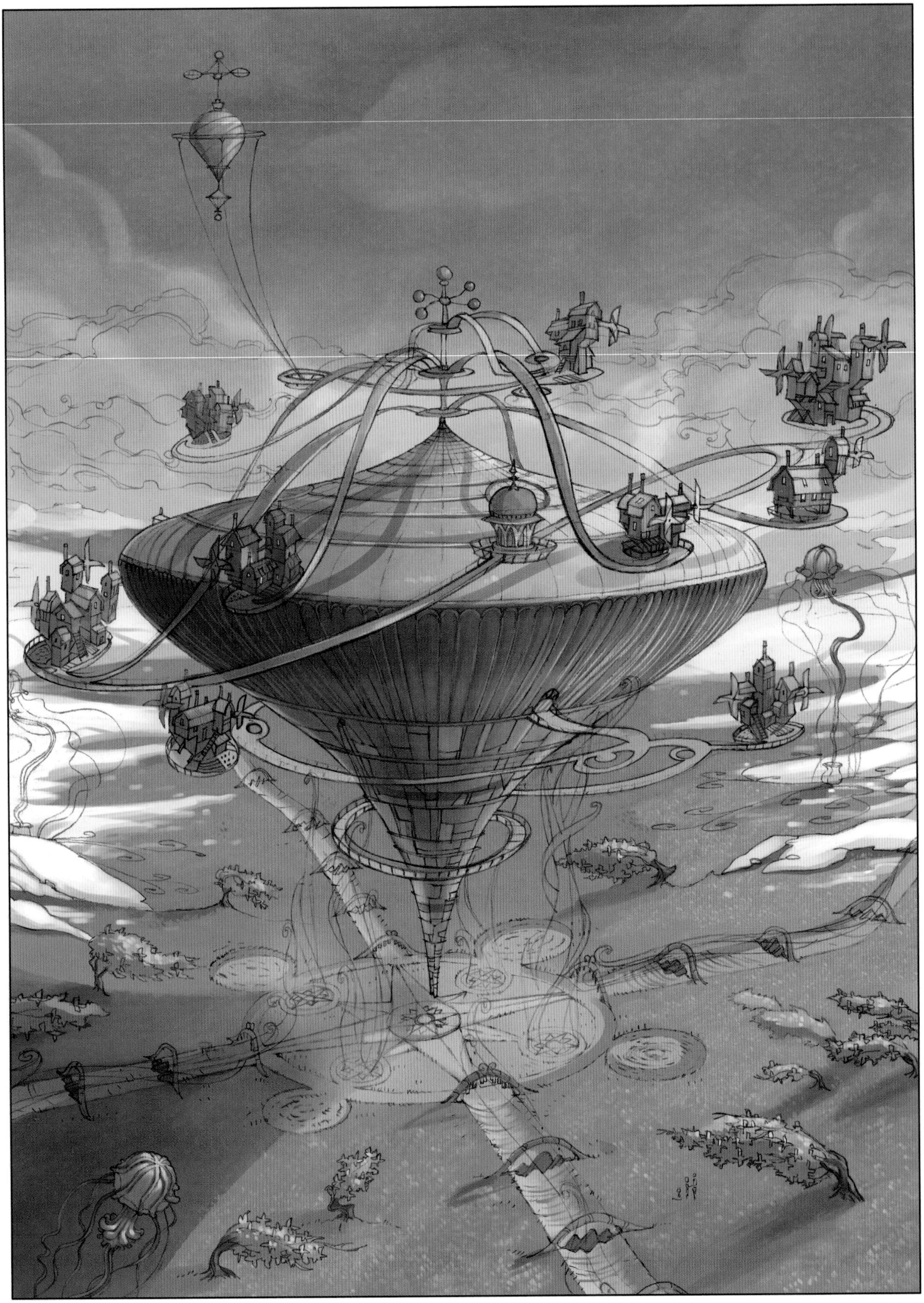

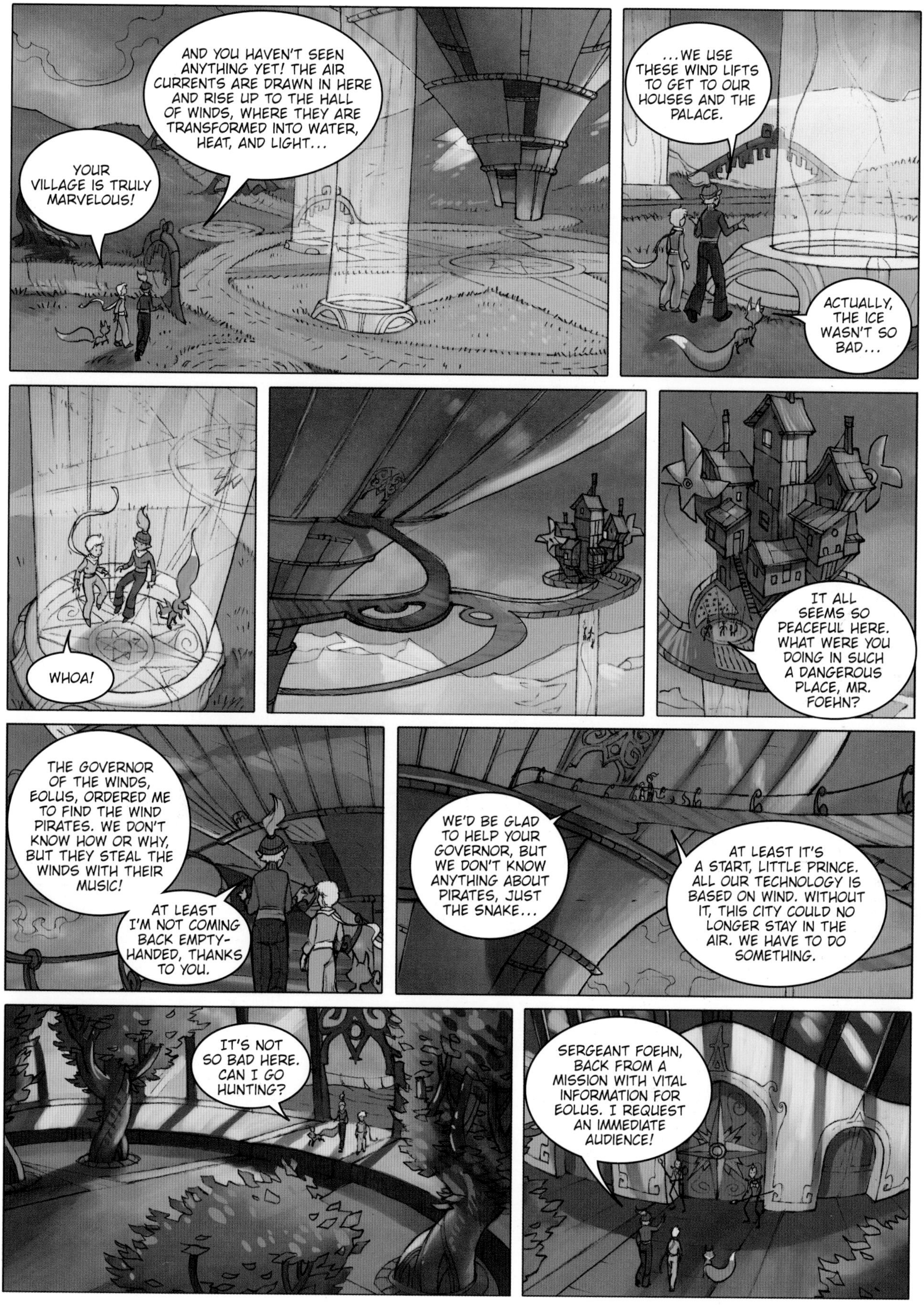
AND YOU HAVEN'T SEEN ANYTHING YET! THE AIR CURRENTS ARE DRAWN IN HERE AND RISE UP TO THE HALL OF WINDS, WHERE THEY ARE TRANSFORMED INTO WATER, HEAT, AND LIGHT...
YOUR VILLAGE IS TRULY MARVELOUS!
...WE USE THESE WIND LIFTS TO GET TO OUR HOUSES AND THE PALACE.
ACTUALLY, THE ICE WASN'T SO BAD...
WHOA!
IT ALL SEEMS SO PEACEFUL HERE. WHAT WERE YOU DOING IN SUCH A DANGEROUS PLACE, MR. FOEHN?
THE GOVERNOR OF THE WINDS, EOLUS, ORDERED ME TO FIND THE WIND PIRATES. WE DON'T KNOW HOW OR WHY, BUT THEY STEAL THE WINDS WITH THEIR MUSIC!
AT LEAST I'M NOT COMING BACK EMPTY-HANDED, THANKS TO YOU.
WE'D BE GLAD TO HELP YOUR GOVERNOR, BUT WE DON'T KNOW ANYTHING ABOUT PIRATES, JUST THE SNAKE...
AT LEAST IT'S A START, LITTLE PRINCE. ALL OUR TECHNOLOGY IS BASED ON WIND. WITHOUT IT, THIS CITY COULD NO LONGER STAY IN THE AIR. WE HAVE TO DO SOMETHING.
IT'S NOT SO BAD HERE. CAN I GO HUNTING?
SERGEANT FOEHN, BACK FROM A MISSION WITH VITAL INFORMATION FOR EOLUS. I REQUEST AN IMMEDIATE AUDIENCE!

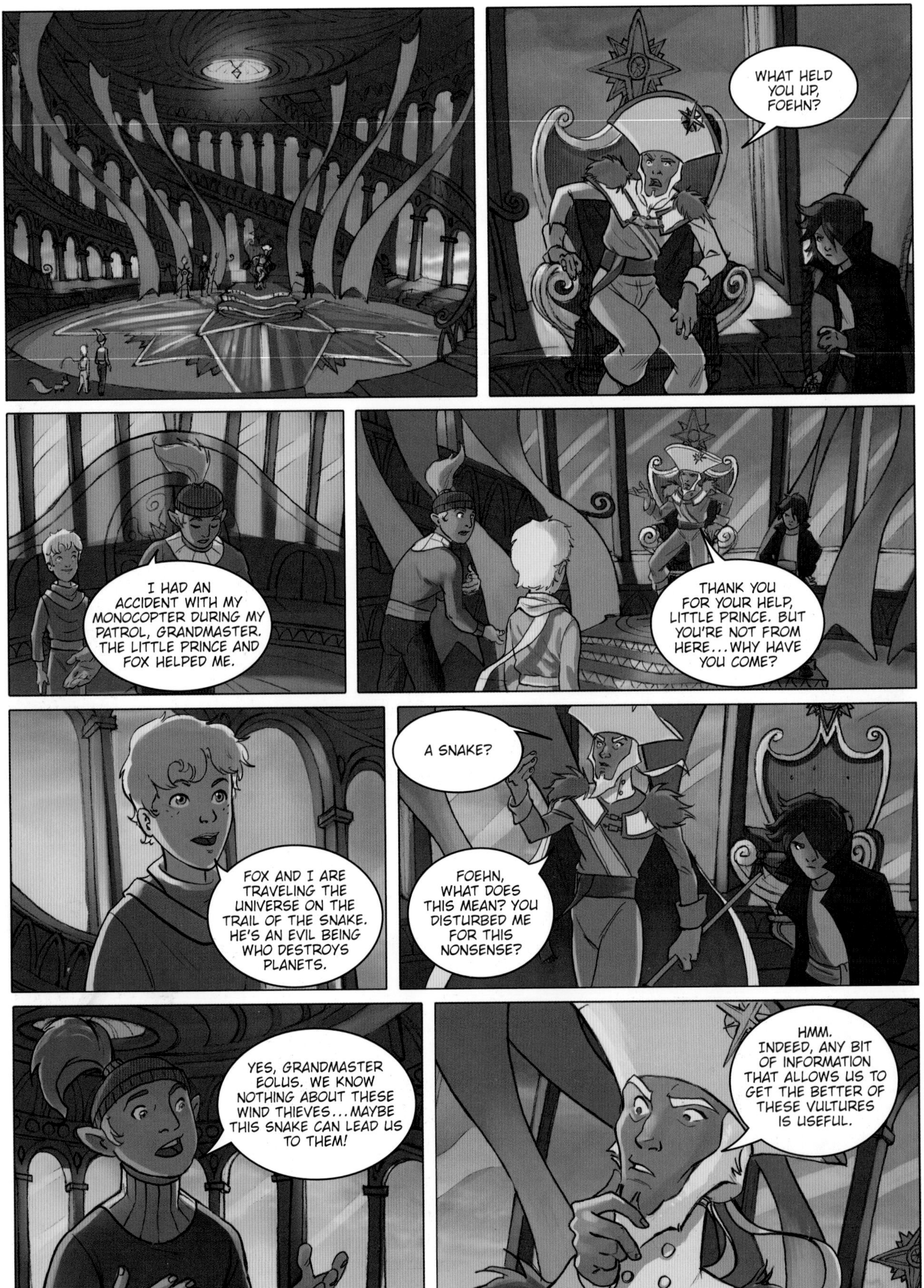
WHAT HELD YOU UP, FOEHN?
I HAD AN ACCIDENT WITH MY MONOCOPTER DURING MY PATROL, GRANDMASTER. THE LITTLE PRINCE AND FOX HELPED ME.
THANK YOU FOR YOUR HELP, LITTLE PRINCE. BUT YOU'RE NOT FROM HERE... WHY HAVE YOU COME?
FOX AND I ARE TRAVELING THE UNIVERSE ON THE TRAIL OF THE SNAKE. HE'S AN EVIL BEING WHO DESTROYS PLANETS.
A SNAKE?
FOEHN, WHAT DOES THIS MEAN? YOU DISTURBED ME FOR THIS NONSENSE?
YES, GRANDMASTER EOLUS. WE KNOW NOTHING ABOUT THESE WIND THIEVES... MAYBE THIS SNAKE CAN LEAD US TO THEM!
HMM. INDEED, ANY BIT OF INFORMATION THAT ALLOWS US TO GET THE BETTER OF THESE VULTURES IS USEFUL.

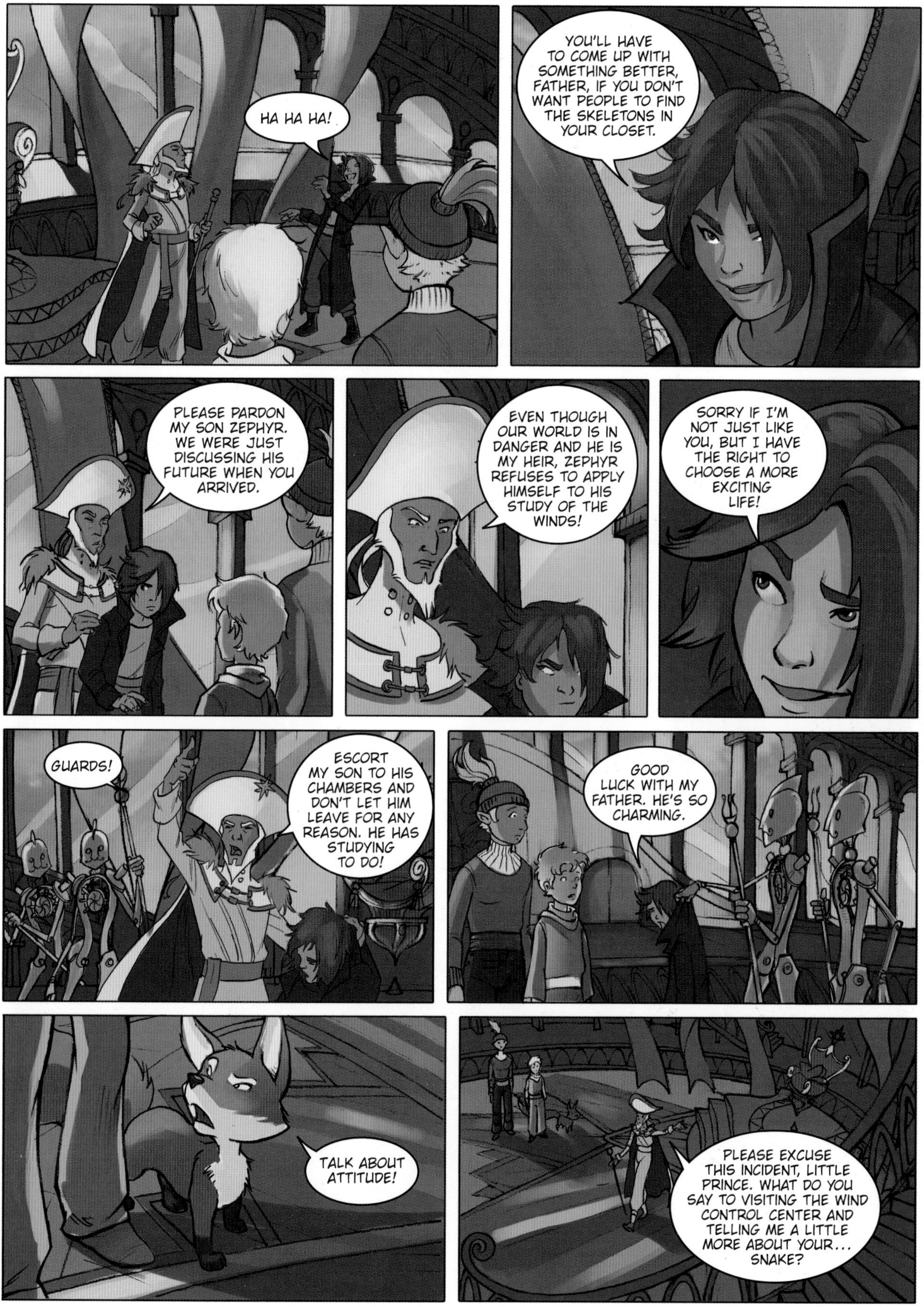
HA HA HA!
YOU'LL HAVE TO COME UP WITH SOMETHING BETTER, FATHER, IF YOU DON'T WANT PEOPLE TO FIND THE SKELETONS IN YOUR CLOSET.
PLEASE PARDON MY SON ZEPHYR. WE WERE JUST DISCUSSING HIS FUTURE WHEN YOU ARRIVED.
EVEN THOUGH OUR WORLD IS IN DANGER AND HE IS MY HEIR, ZEPHYR REFUSES TO APPLY HIMSELF TO HIS STUDY OF THE WINDS!
SORRY IF I'M NOT JUST LIKE YOU, BUT I HAVE THE RIGHT TO CHOOSE A MORE EXCITING LIFE!
GUARDS!
ESCORT MY SON TO HIS CHAMBERS AND DON'T LET HIM LEAVE FOR ANY REASON. HE HAS STUDYING TO DO!
GOOD LUCK WITH MY FATHER. HE'S SO CHARMING.
TALK ABOUT ATTITUDE!
PLEASE EXCUSE THIS INCIDENT, LITTLE PRINCE. WHAT DO YOU SAY TO VISITING THE WIND CONTROL CENTER AND TELLING ME A LITTLE MORE ABOUT YOUR... SNAKE?

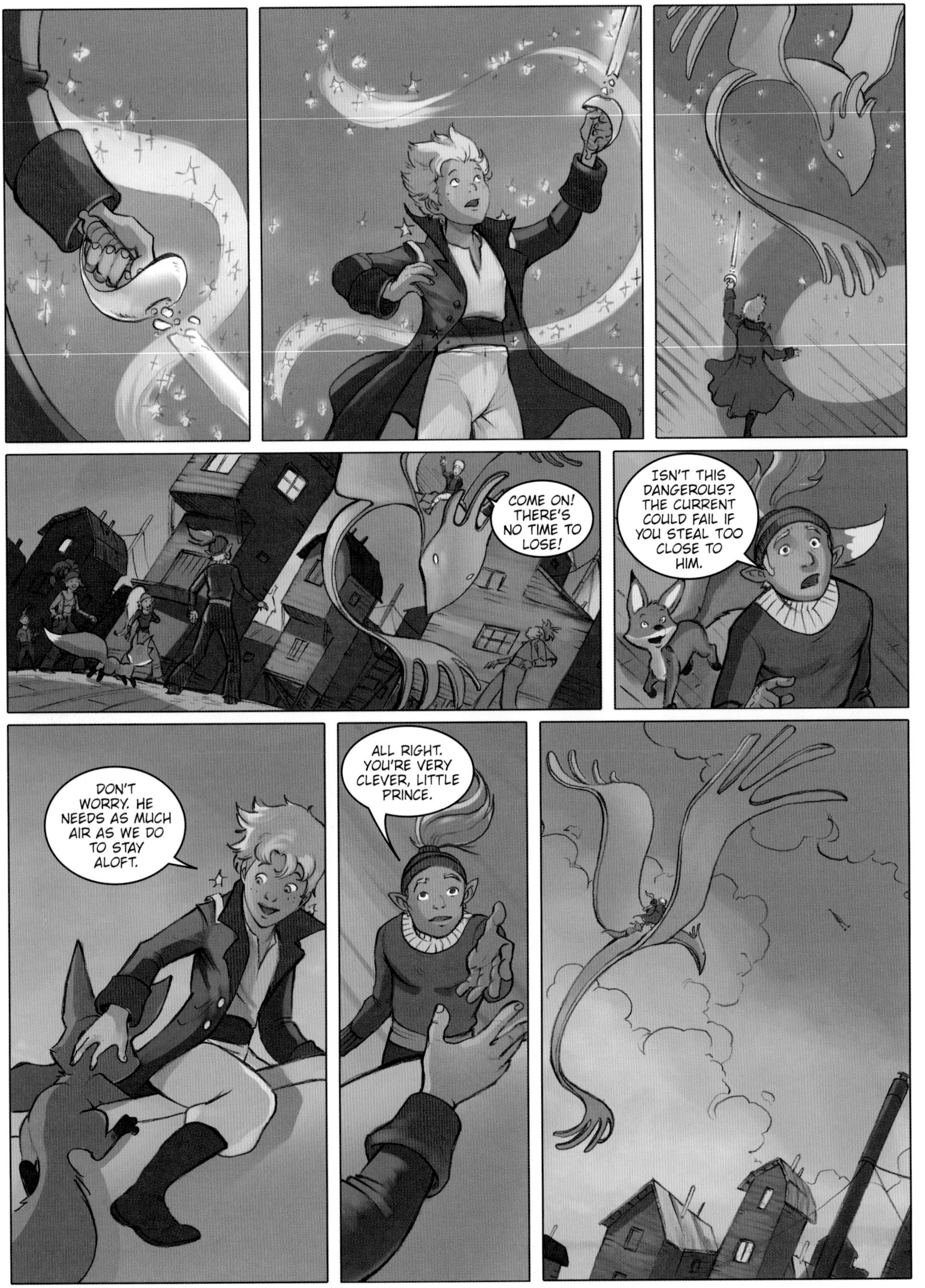
COME ON! THERE'S NO TIME TO LOSE!
ISN'T THIS DANGEROUS? THE CURRENT COULD FAIL IF YOU STEAL TOO CLOSE TO HIM.
DON'T WORRY. HE NEEDS AS MUCH AIR AS WE DO TO STAY ALOFT.
ALL RIGHT. YOU'RE VERY CLEVER, LITTLE PRINCE.

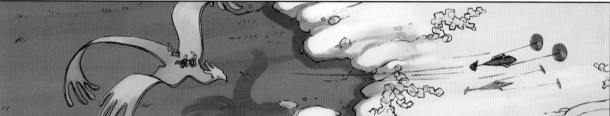

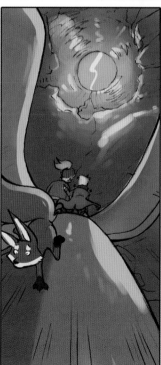

WE...WE CAN'T GO ANY FARTHER. HE'S HEADED FOR THE FROZEN PLAIN. NO ONE'S EVER COME BACK FROM THERE!

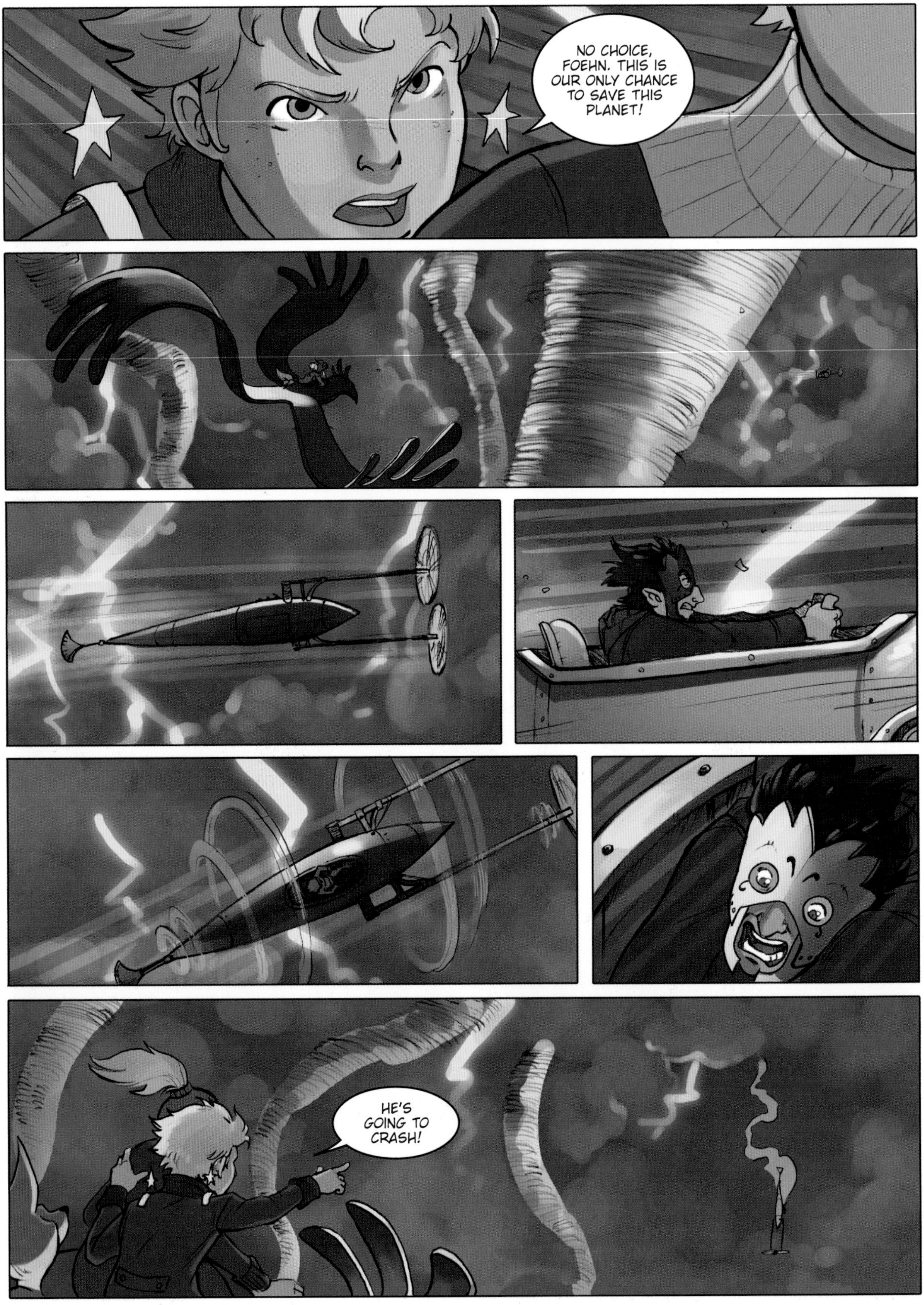
NO CHOICE, FOEHN. THIS IS OUR ONLY CHANCE TO SAVE THIS PLANET!
HE'S GOING TO CRASH!

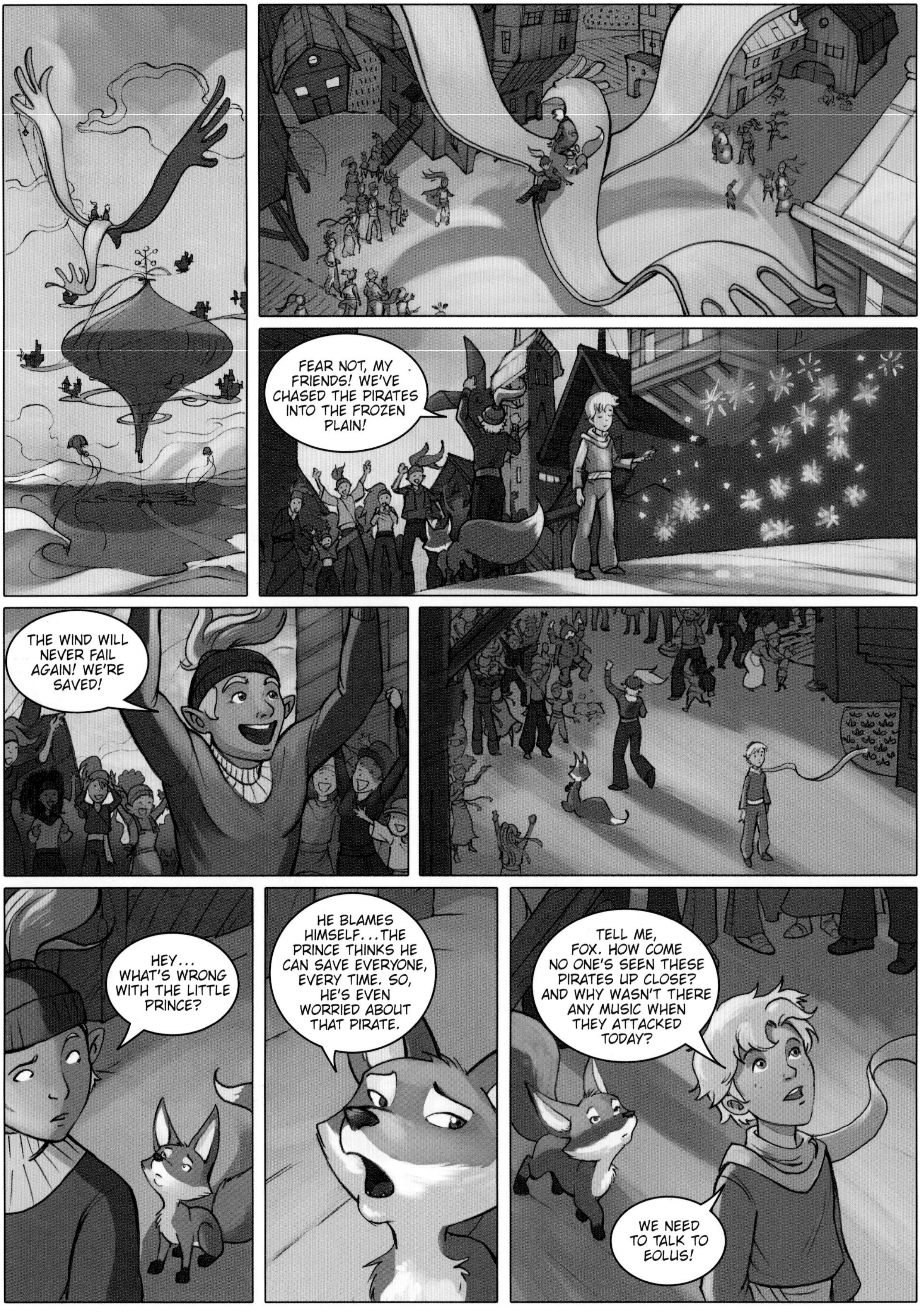
FEAR NOT, MY FRIENDS! WE'VE CHASED THE PIRATES INTO THE FROZEN PLAIN!
THE WIND WILL NEVER FAIL AGAIN! WE'RE SAVED!
HEY... WHAT'S WRONG WITH THE LITTLE PRINCE?
HE BLAMES HIMSELF...THE PRINCE THINKS HE CAN SAVE EVERYONE, EVERY TIME. SO, HE'S EVEN WORRIED ABOUT THAT PIRATE.
TELL ME, FOX. HOW COME NO ONE'S SEEN THESE PIRATES UP CLOSE? AND WHY WASN'T THERE ANY MUSIC WHEN THEY ATTACKED TODAY?
WE NEED TO TALK TO EOLUS!

23

25

26

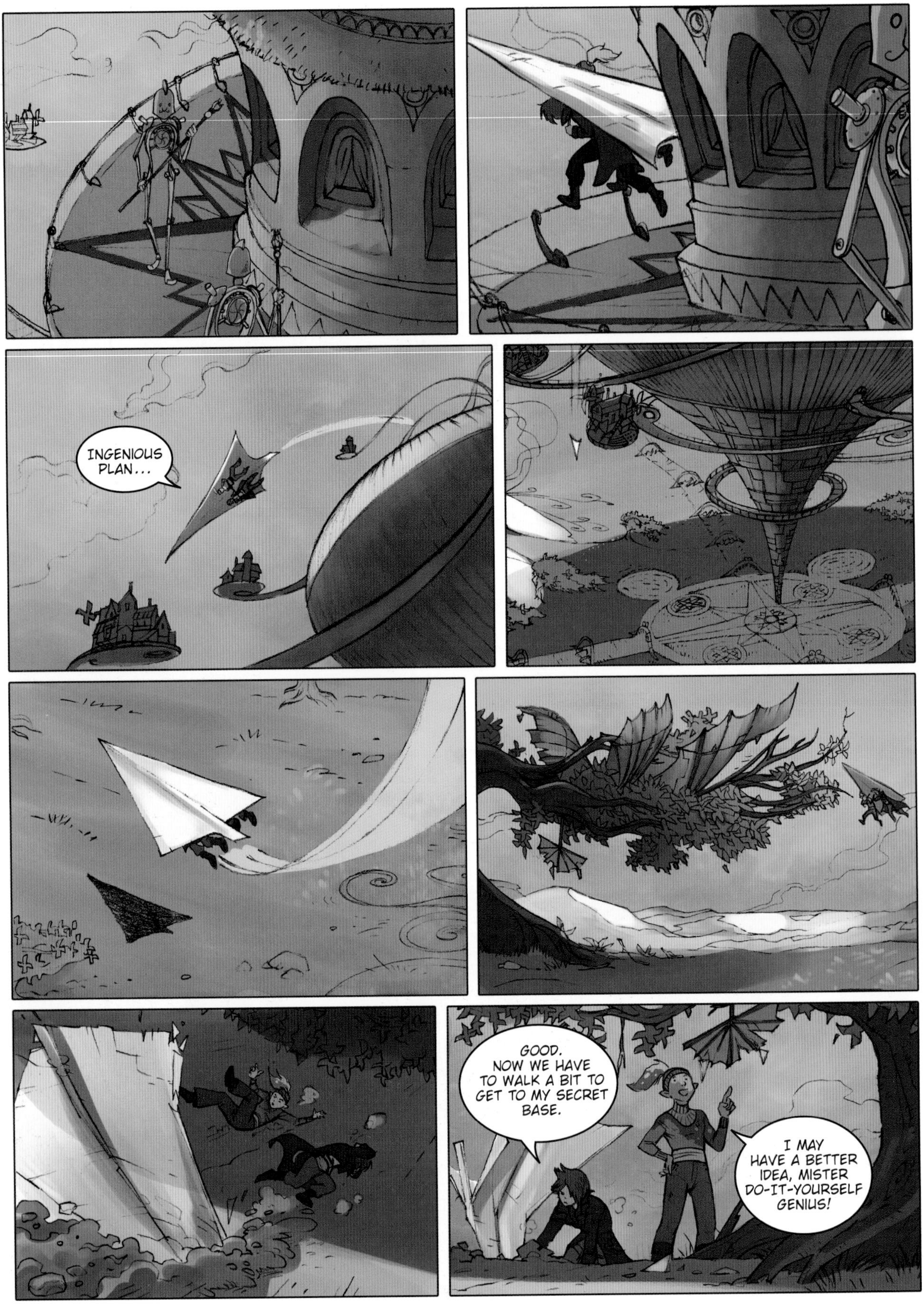
INGENIOUS PLAN...
GOOD. NOW WE HAVE TO WALK A BIT TO GET TO MY SECRET BASE.
I MAY HAVE A BETTER IDEA, MISTER DO-IT-YOURSELF GENIUS!

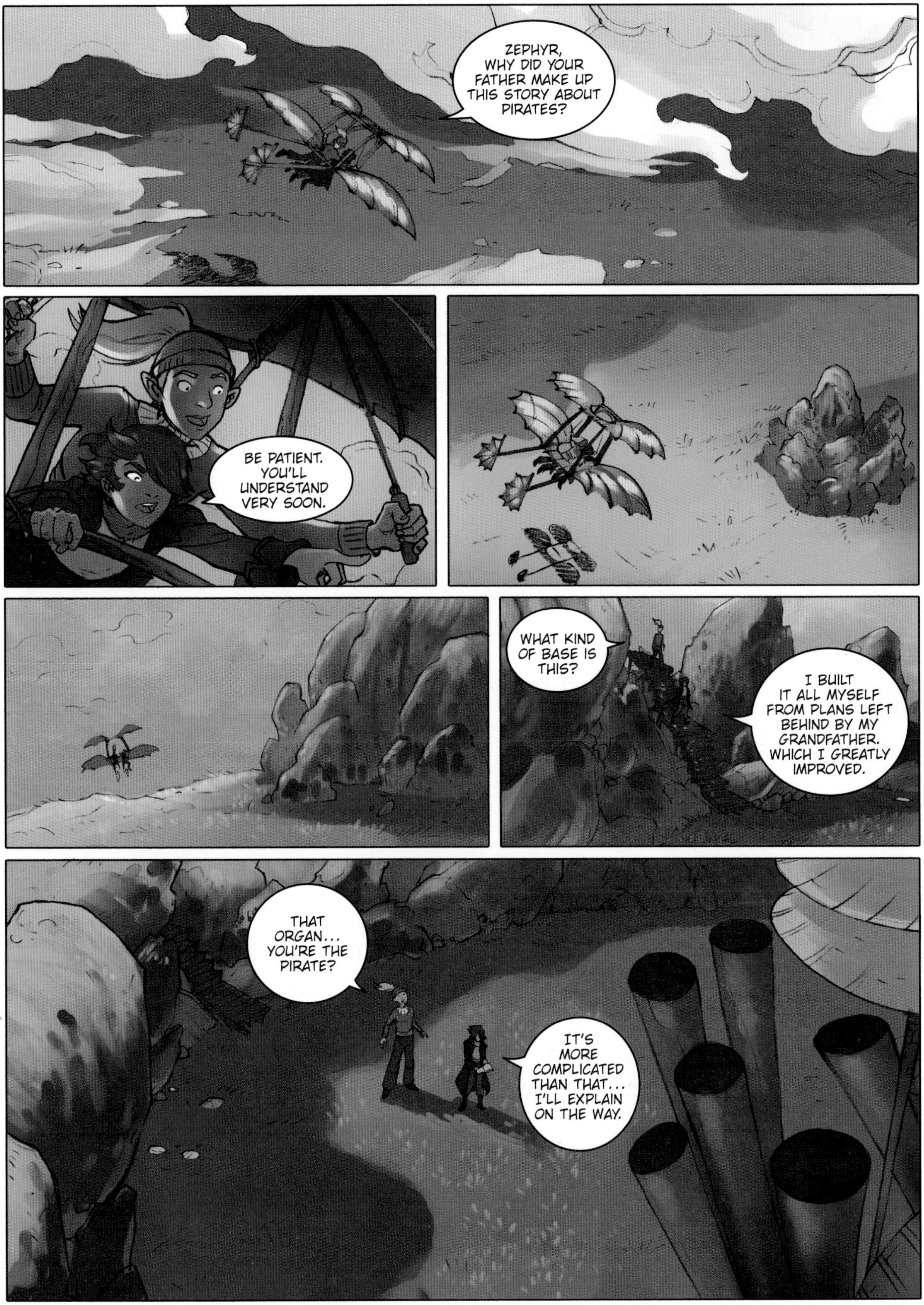
ZEPHYR, WHY DID YOUR FATHER MAKE UP THIS STORY ABOUT PIRATES?
BE PATIENT. YOU'LL UNDERSTAND VERY SOON.
WHAT KIND OF BASE IS THIS?
I BUILT IT ALL MYSELF FROM PLANS LEFT BEHIND BY MY GRANDFATHER. WHICH I GREATLY IMPROVED.
THAT ORGAN... YOU'RE THE PIRATE?
IT'S MORE COMPLICATED THAN THAT... I'LL EXPLAIN ON THE WAY.

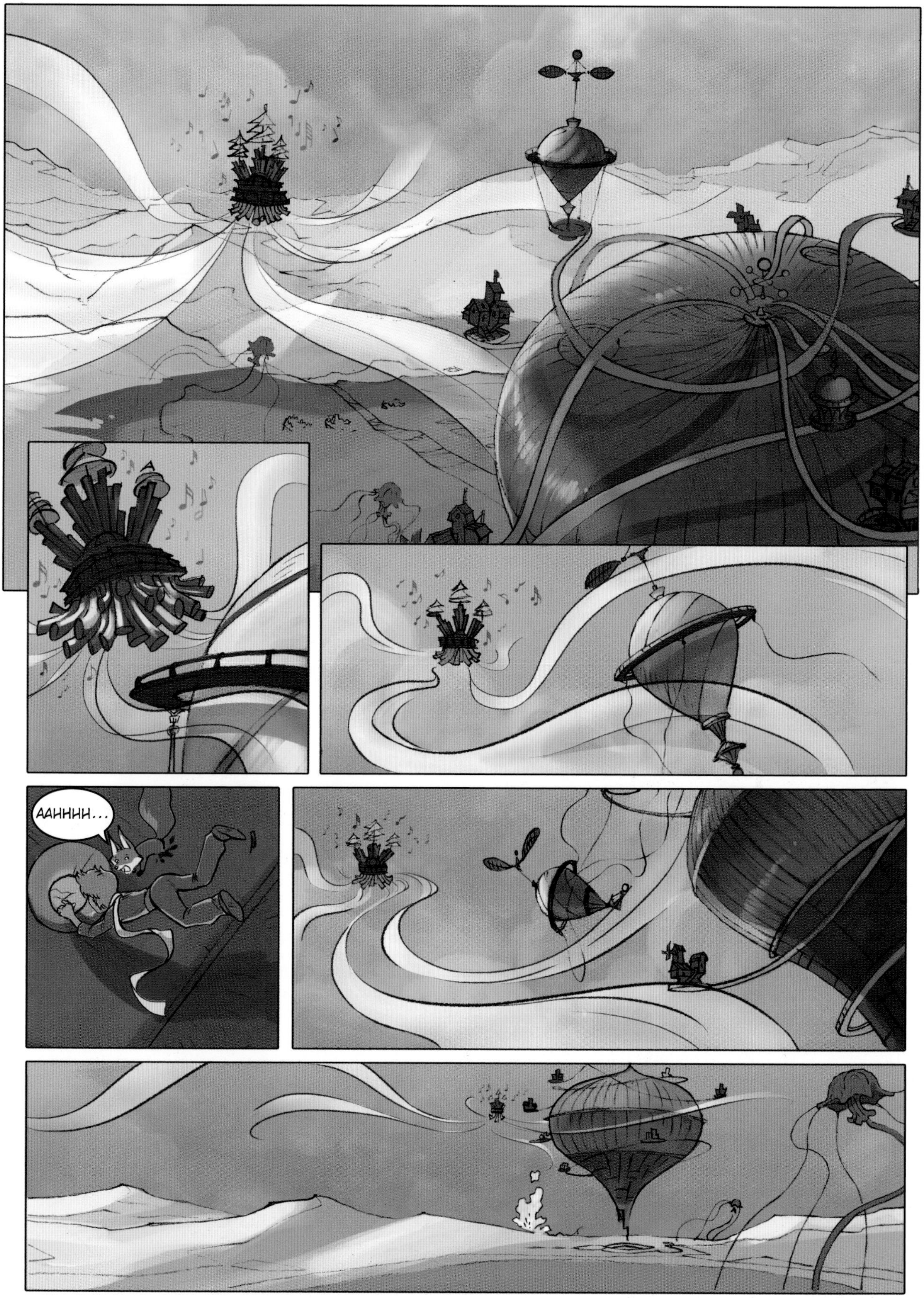
AAHHHH...

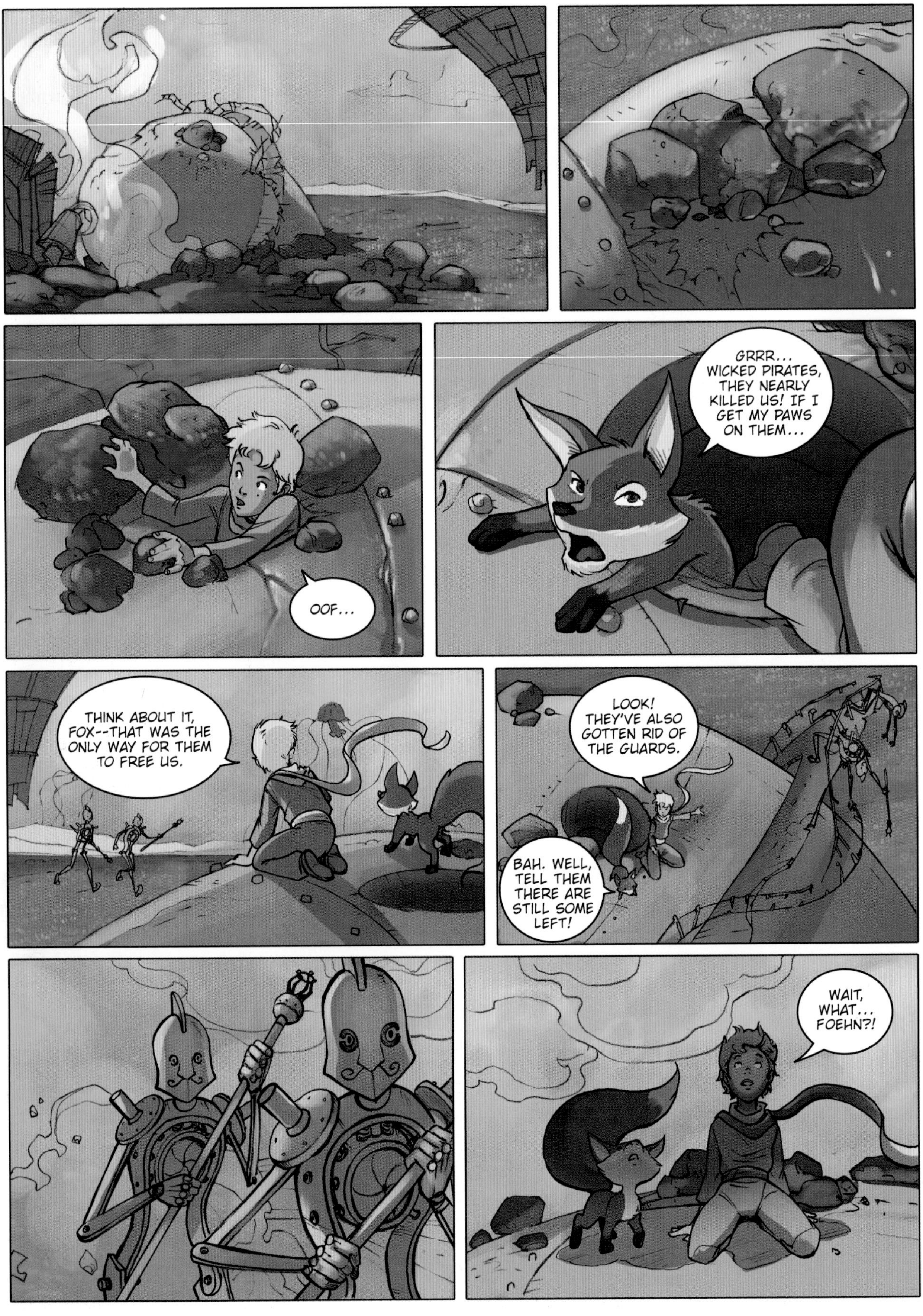
OOF...
GRRR... WICKED PIRATES, THEY NEARLY KILLED US! IF I GET MY PAWS ON THEM...
THINK ABOUT IT, FOX--THAT WAS THE ONLY WAY FOR THEM TO FREE US.
LOOK! THEY'VE ALSO GOTTEN RID OF THE GUARDS.
BAH. WELL, TELL THEM THERE ARE STILL SOME LEFT!
WAIT, WHAT... FOEHN?!

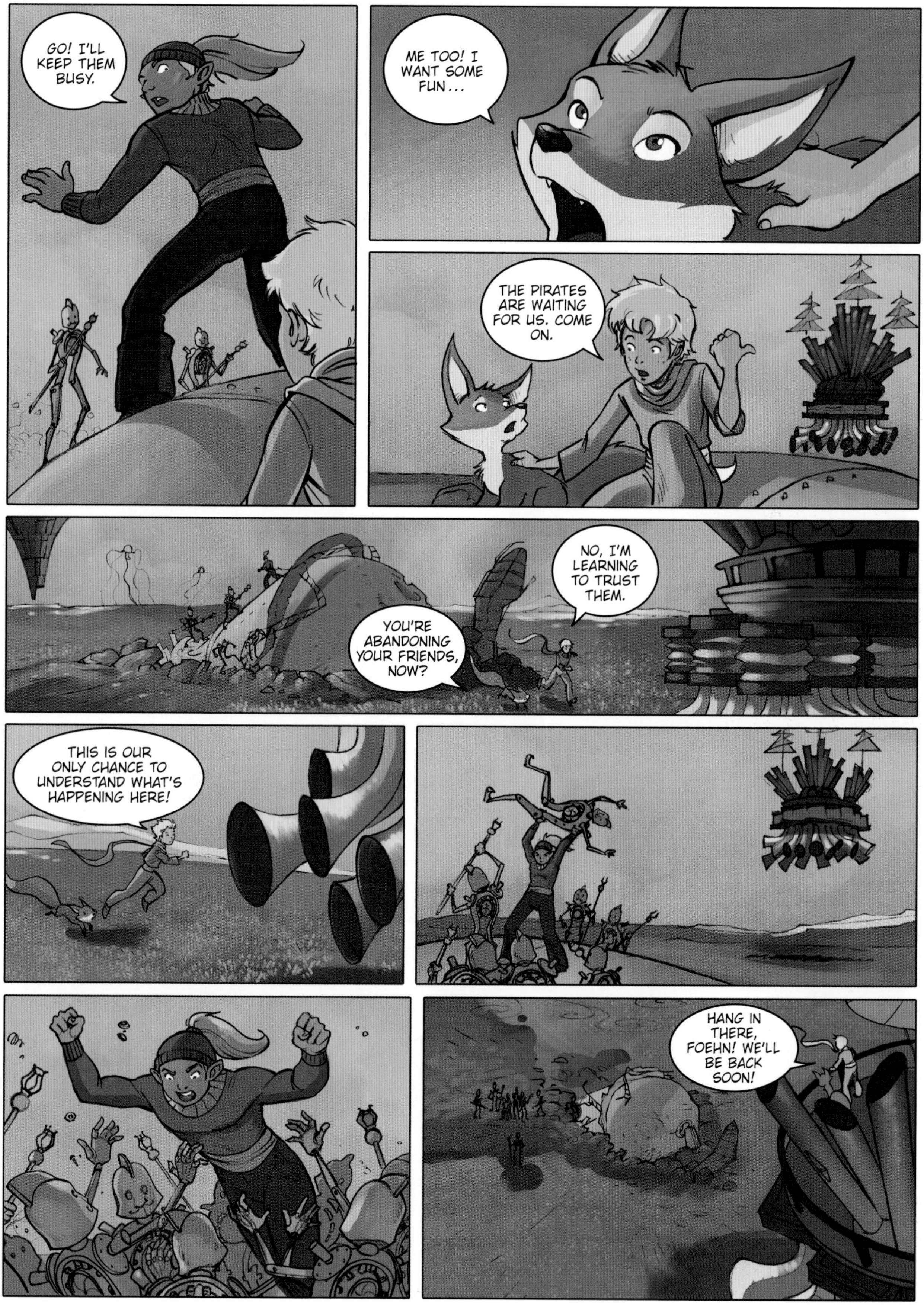
GO! I'LL KEEP THEM BUSY.
ME TOO! I WANT SOME FUN...
THE PIRATES ARE WAITING FOR US. COME ON.
YOU'RE ABANDONING YOUR FRIENDS, NOW?
NO, I'M LEARNING TO TRUST THEM.
THIS IS OUR ONLY CHANCE TO UNDERSTAND WHAT'S HAPPENING HERE!
HANG IN THERE, FOEHN! WE'LL BE BACK SOON!

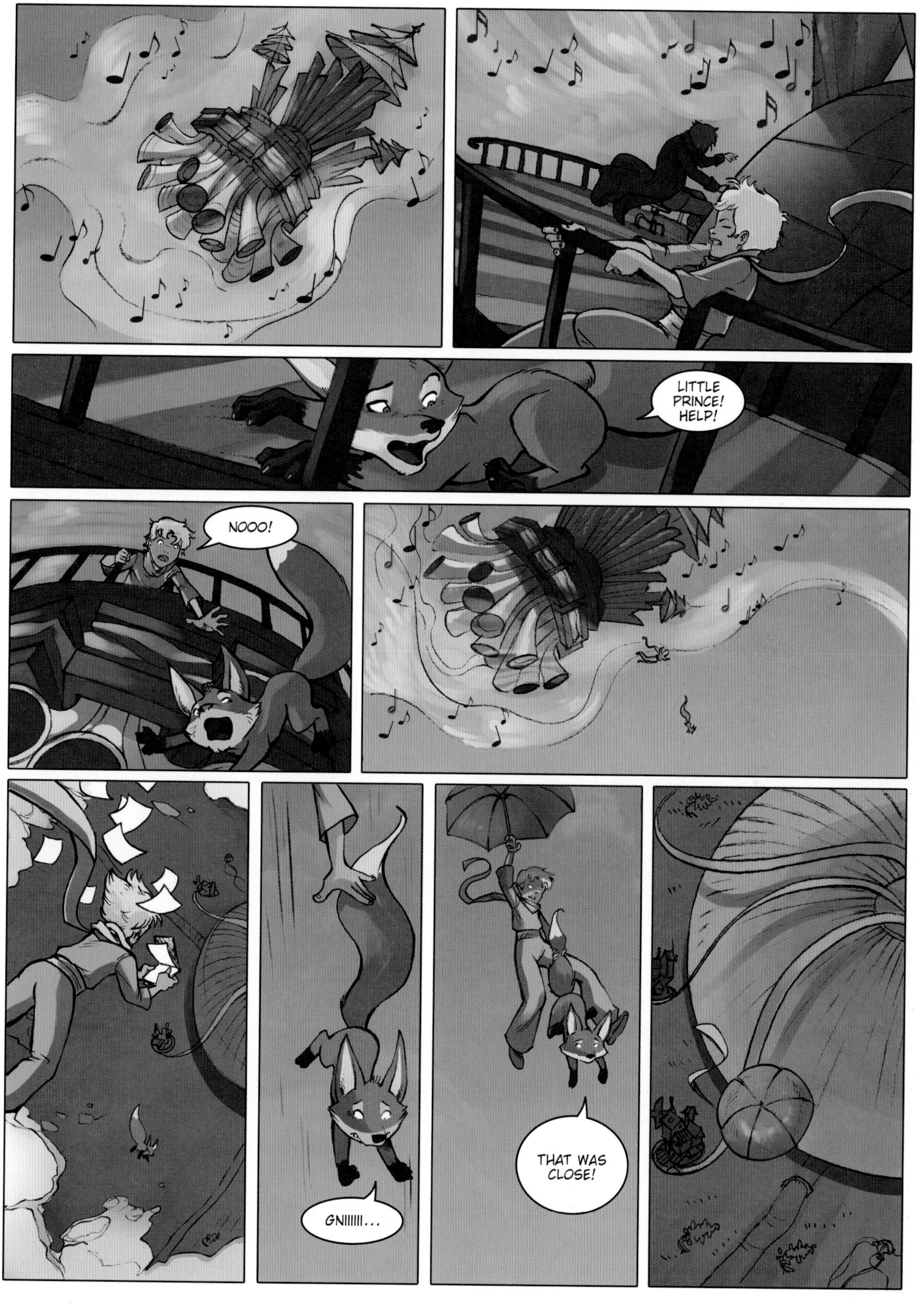

LITTLE PRINCE! HELP!
NOOO!
GNIIIIII...
THAT WAS CLOSE!

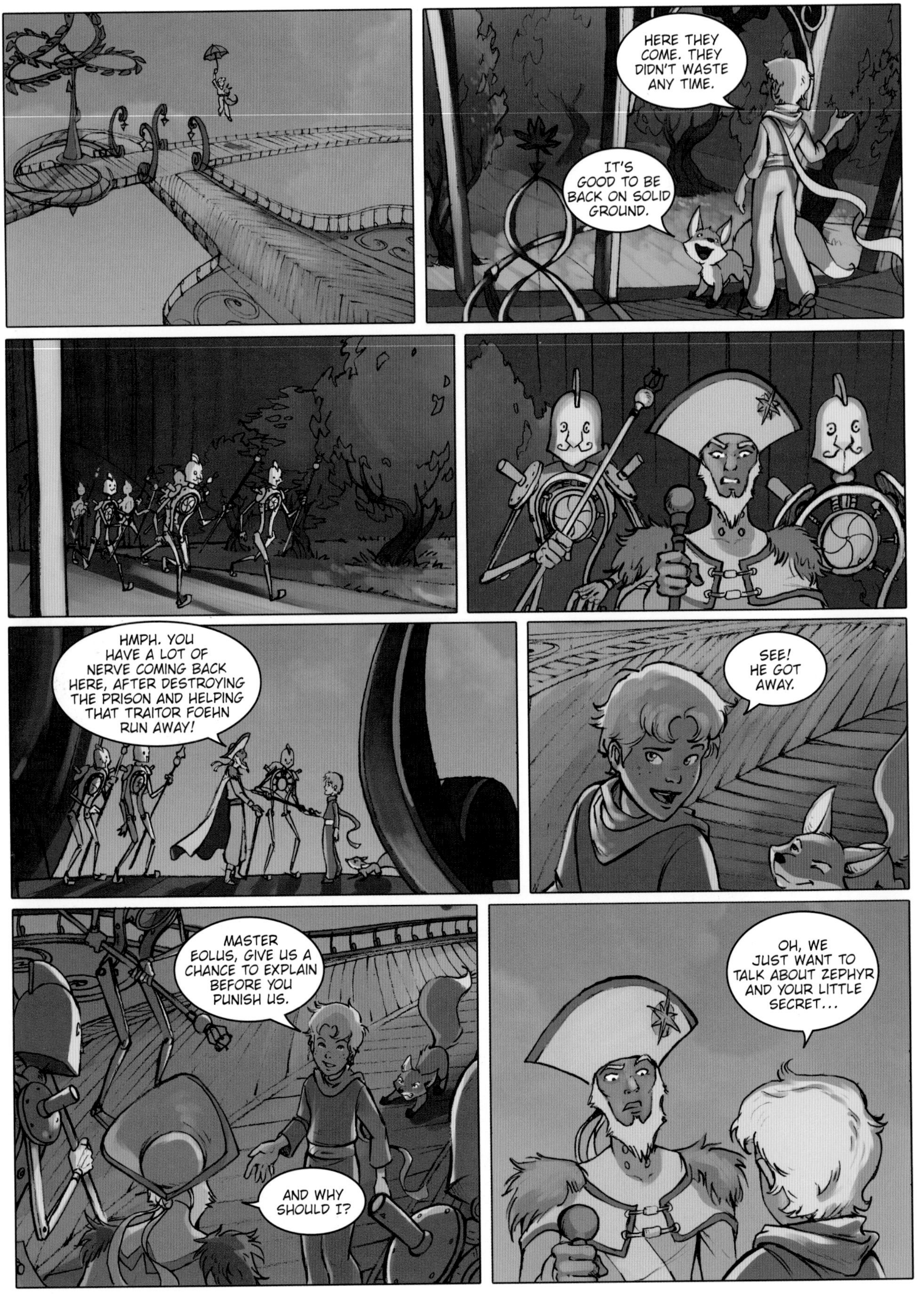
HERE THEY COME. THEY DIDN'T WASTE ANY TIME.
IT'S GOOD TO BE BACK ON SOLID GROUND.
HMPH. YOU HAVE A LOT OF NERVE COMING BACK HERE, AFTER DESTROYING THE PRISON AND HELPING THAT TRAITOR FOEHN RUN AWAY!
SEE! HE GOT AWAY.
MASTER EOLUS, GIVE US A CHANCE TO EXPLAIN BEFORE YOU PUNISH US.
AND WHY SHOULD I?
OH, WE JUST WANT TO TALK ABOUT ZEPHYR AND YOUR LITTLE SECRET...

43

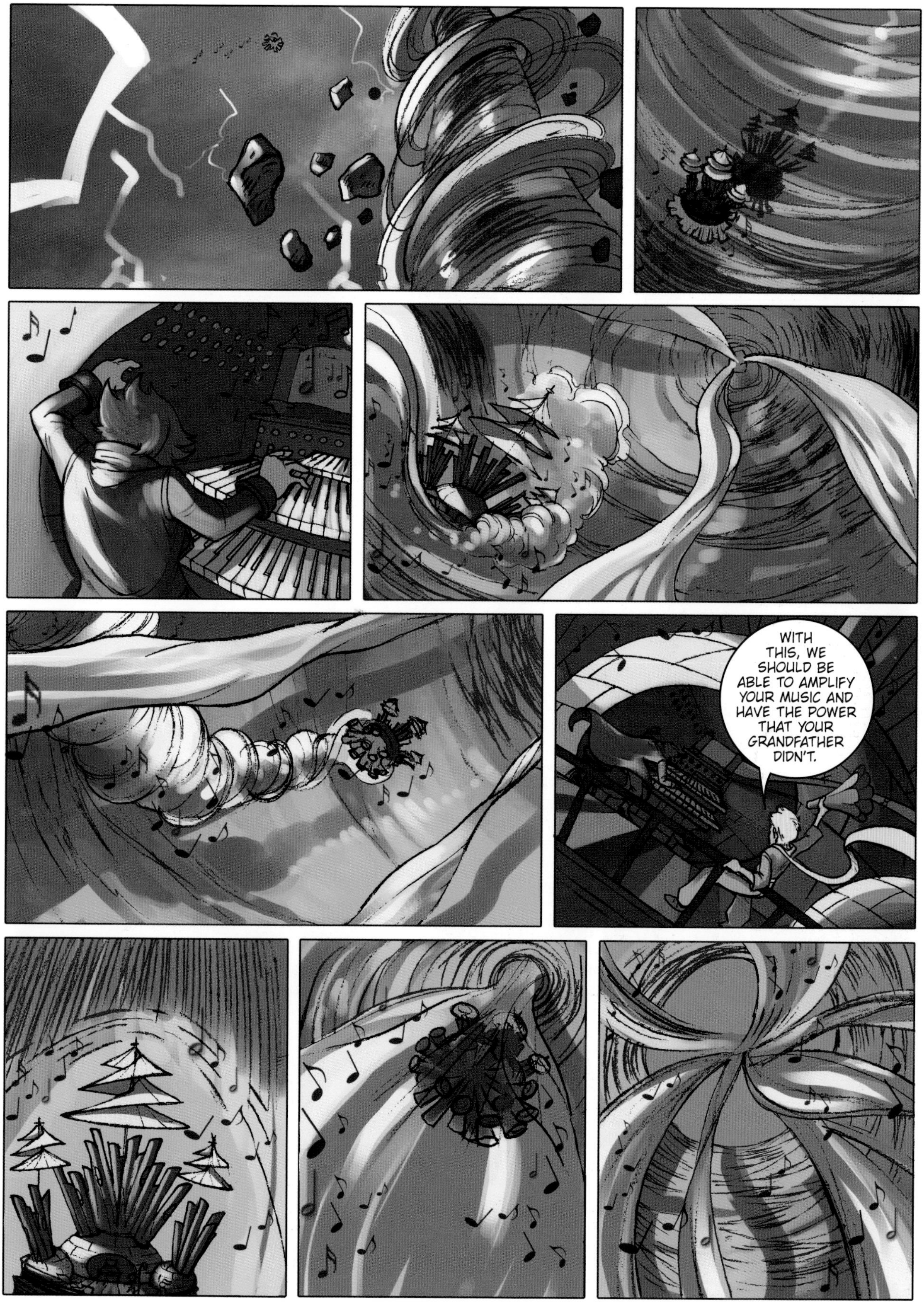
WITH THIS, WE SHOULD BE ABLE TO AMPLIFY YOUR MUSIC AND HAVE THE POWER THAT YOUR GRANDFATHER DIDN'T.

THE END

The Little Prince

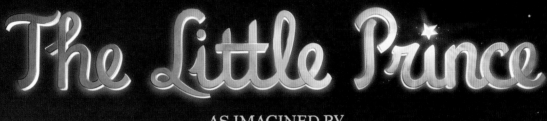

AS IMAGINED BY

MOEBIUS

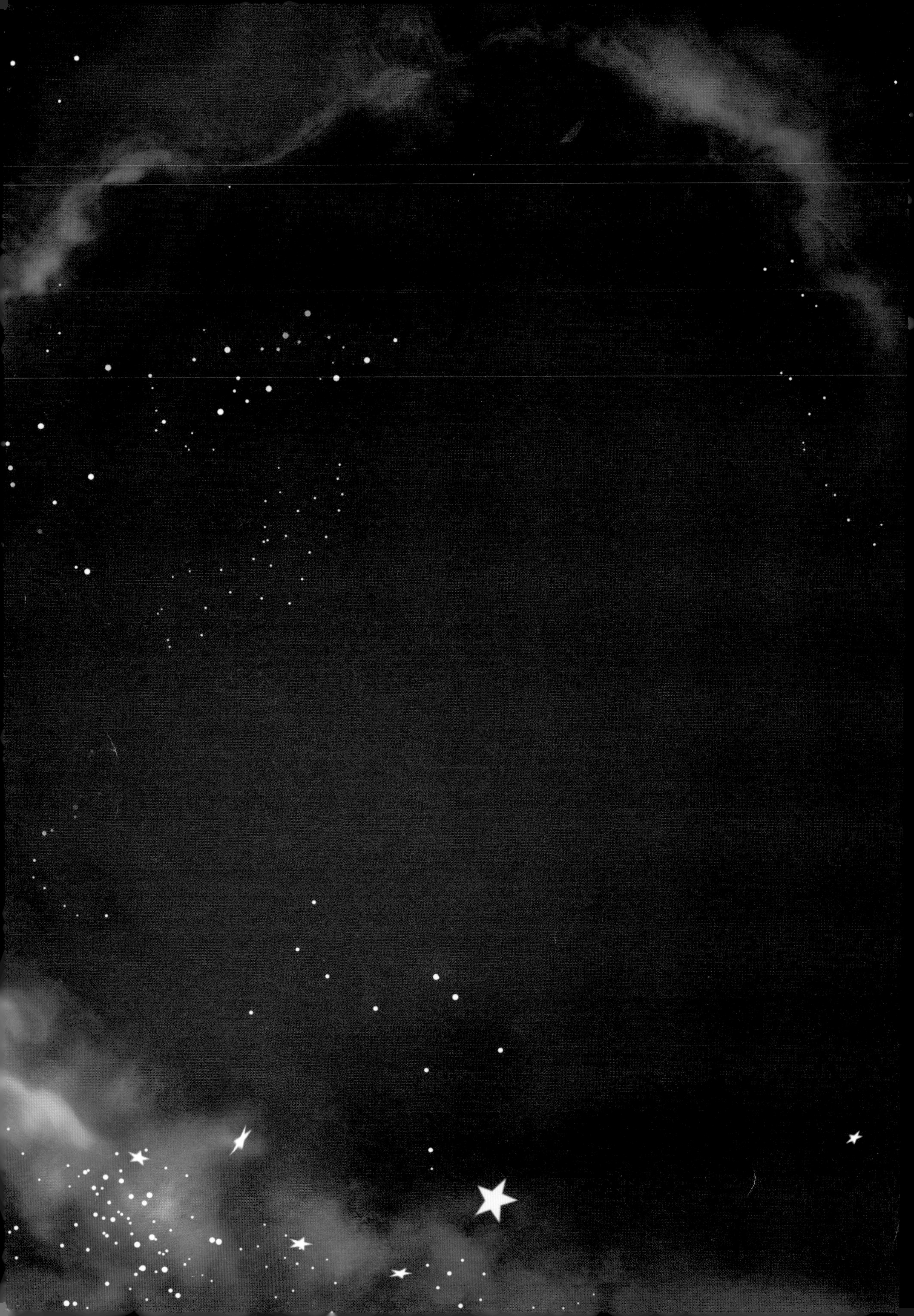

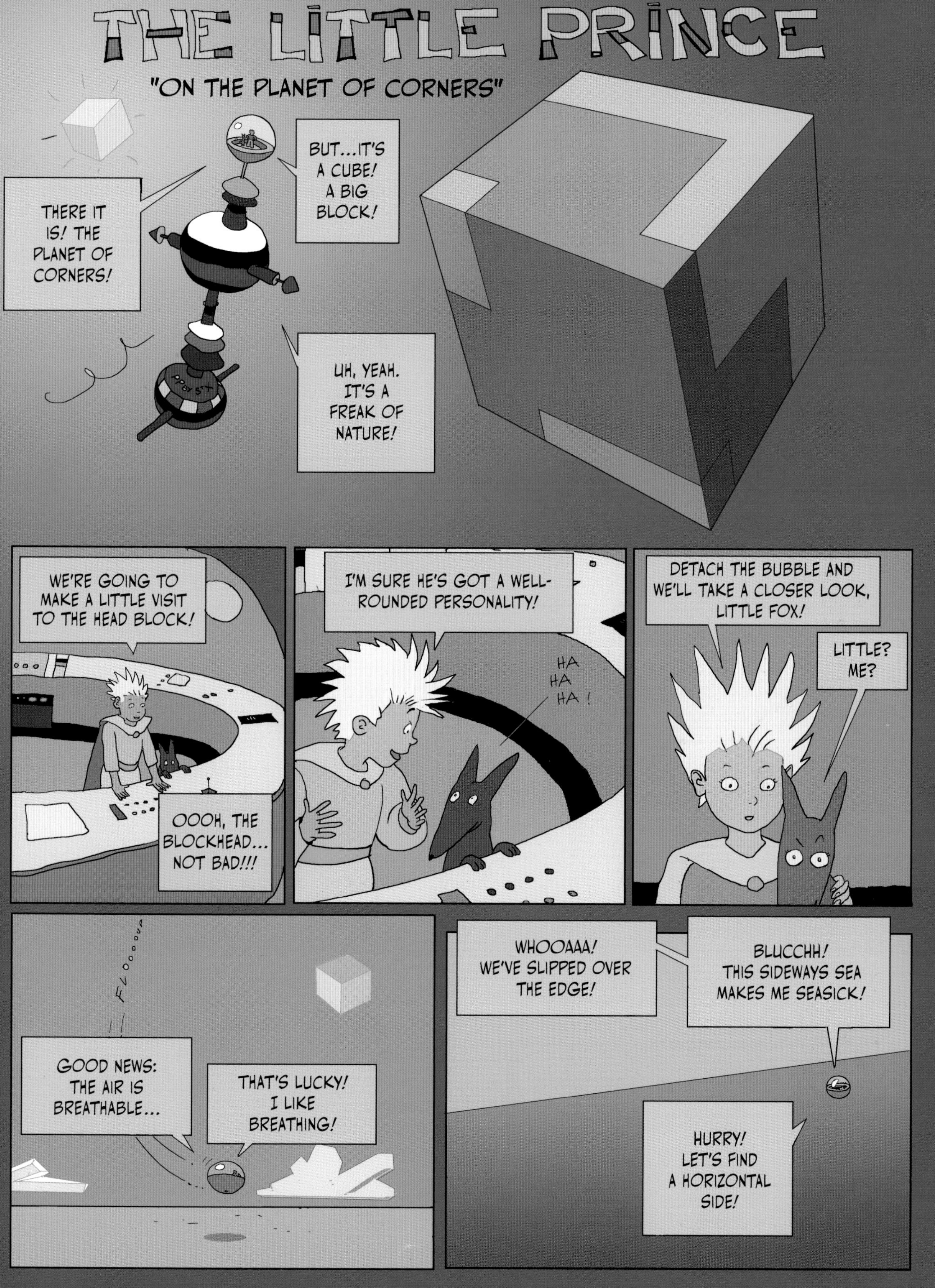
THE LITTLE PRINCE
"ON THE PLANET OF CORNERS"
THERE IT IS! THE PLANET OF CORNERS!
BUT...IT'S A CUBE! A BIG BLOCK!
UH, YEAH. IT'S A FREAK OF NATURE!
WE'RE GOING TO MAKE A LITTLE VISIT TO THE HEAD BLOCK!
OOOH, THE BLOCKHEAD... NOT BAD!!!
I'M SURE HE'S GOT A WELL-ROUNDED PERSONALITY!
HA HA HA!
DETACH THE BUBBLE AND WE'LL TAKE A CLOSER LOOK, LITTLE FOX!
LITTLE? ME?
FLOOOOOP
GOOD NEWS: THE AIR IS BREATHABLE...
THAT'S LUCKY! I LIKE BREATHING!
WHOOAAA! WE'VE SLIPPED OVER THE EDGE!
BLUCCHH! THIS SIDEWAYS SEA MAKES ME SEASICK!
HURRY! LET'S FIND A HORIZONTAL SIDE!

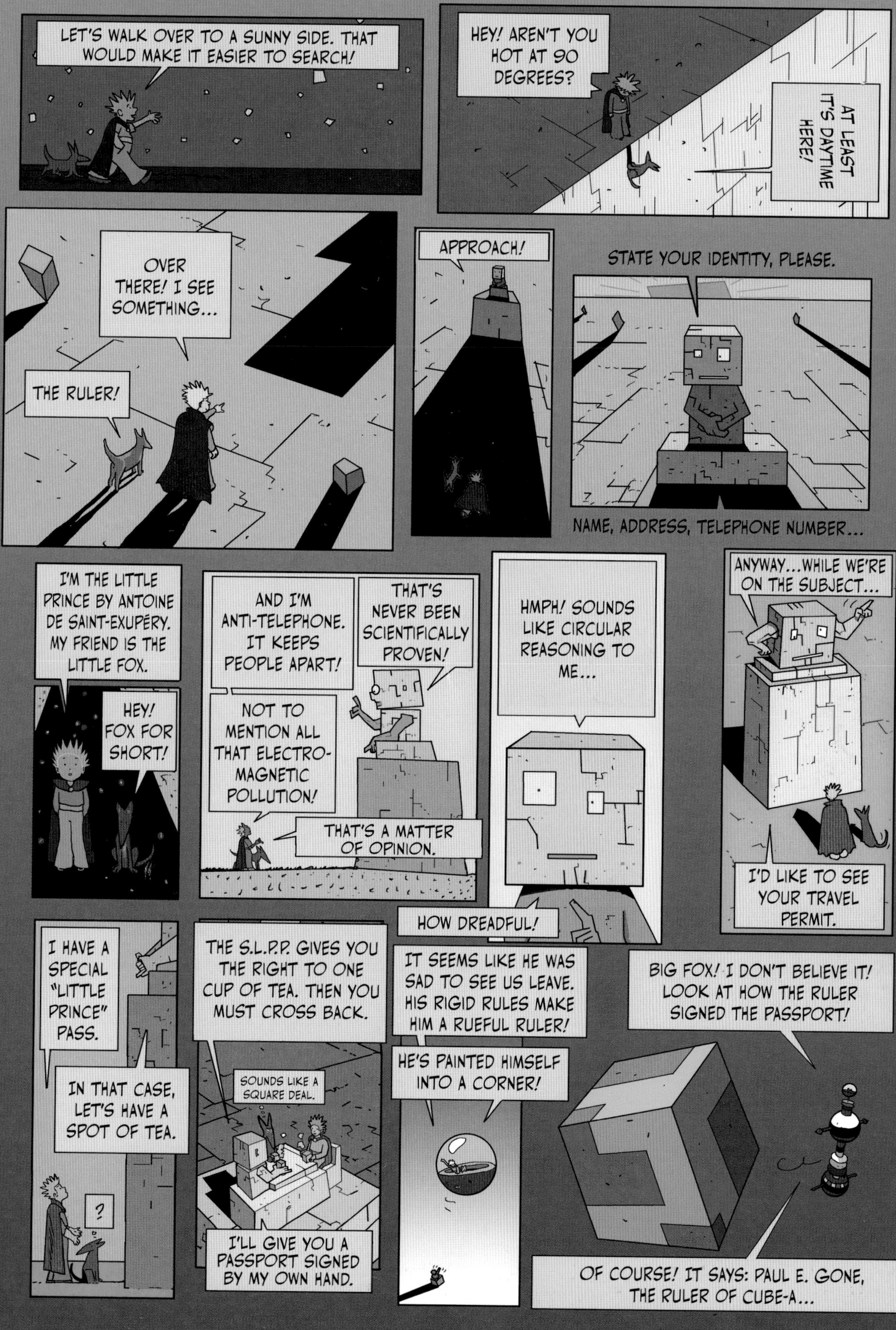
LET'S WALK OVER TO A SUNNY SIDE. THAT WOULD MAKE IT EASIER TO SEARCH!
HEY! AREN'T YOU HOT AT 90 DEGREES?
AT LEAST IT'S DAYTIME HERE!
OVER THERE! I SEE SOMETHING...
THE RULER!
APPROACH!
STATE YOUR IDENTITY, PLEASE.
NAME, ADDRESS, TELEPHONE NUMBER...
I'M THE LITTLE PRINCE BY ANTOINE DE SAINT-EXUPÉRY. MY FRIEND IS THE LITTLE FOX.
HEY! FOX FOR SHORT!
AND I'M ANTI-TELEPHONE. IT KEEPS PEOPLE APART!
THAT'S NEVER BEEN SCIENTIFICALLY PROVEN!
NOT TO MENTION ALL THAT ELECTRO-MAGNETIC POLLUTION!
THAT'S A MATTER OF OPINION.
HMPH! SOUNDS LIKE CIRCULAR REASONING TO ME...
HOW DREADFUL!
ANYWAY...WHILE WE'RE ON THE SUBJECT...
I'D LIKE TO SEE YOUR TRAVEL PERMIT.
I HAVE A SPECIAL "LITTLE PRINCE" PASS.
IN THAT CASE, LET'S HAVE A SPOT OF TEA.
?
THE S.L.P.P. GIVES YOU THE RIGHT TO ONE CUP OF TEA. THEN YOU MUST CROSS BACK.
SOUNDS LIKE A SQUARE DEAL.
I'LL GIVE YOU A PASSPORT SIGNED BY MY OWN HAND.
IT SEEMS LIKE HE WAS SAD TO SEE US LEAVE. HIS RIGID RULES MAKE HIM A RUEFUL RULER!
HE'S PAINTED HIMSELF INTO A CORNER!
BIG FOX! I DON'T BELIEVE IT! LOOK AT HOW THE RULER SIGNED THE PASSPORT!
OF COURSE! IT SAYS: PAUL E. GONE, THE RULER OF CUBE-A...

ANTOINE DE SAINT-EXUPÉRY
Aviator • Author • Adventurer • Hero

Antoine de Saint-Exupéry, author of the novel *The Little Prince* on which these new adventures are based, was born on June 29, 1900, in Lyon, France. He was the third of five children: Marie-Madeleine, Simone, Antoine, François, and Gabrielle. It was when he was twelve years old, during his summer break from boarding school, that airplanes and flying first made a huge impression on him.

In 1920, he was accepted into the École des Beaux-Arts in Paris to study architecture, but the next year he joined the Second Aviation Regiment of the armed forces and received his pilot's license. In 1922, he had his first plane crash, and suffered a head fracture. He had to leave the armed forces and work at different jobs on the ground to earn a living.

By May of 1926, Saint-Exupéry was able to fly again. He delivered airmail, which was a new and sometimes dangerous profession, on routes from France to Senegal and all the way to South America. That was where, in 1931, he met and married Consuelo Suncin.

From 1933 to 1938, Saint-Exupéry was very busy. He traveled to North Africa and Indochina, and attempted to break the flight speed record from Paris to Saigon, Vietnam—during which his plane crashed again. It went down in the middle of the Sahara Desert. After his recovery, his life became even busier. He wrote newspaper reports in Spain on the Spanish Civil War, scouted airplane routes between Casablanca and Timbuktu, wrote a screenplay, registered several patents, and traveled to the United States. In 1939, with the start of World War II, he returned to France and talked his way into a job as a high-risk reconnaissance pilot for the French Air Force. But this only lasted until France reached an armistice agreement with Germany.

In December 1940, Saint-Exupéry returned to visit friends in New York, where he finally began work on *The Little Prince.* The story is narrated by a pilot who has crashed his plane into the Sahara Desert. He meets a little prince visiting from a faraway asteroid. Along the way, the prince also meets Fox and Snake. By late 1942, after spending the spring and summer writing and illustrating, Saint-Exupéry had completed his novel, and in April 1943 it was published in his native language of French *(Le Petit Prince)* and in English.

Saint-Exupéry was eager to return to the war. He decided to join the Free French Forces in Algeria, who were continuing the fight against the Axis powers. Because of his age, at first he had a hard time convincing them to let him fly. He was authorized to fly five dangerous missions. In fact, he flew eight. On July 31, 1944, Saint-Exupéry went on a scouting flight to prepare for military landings in the south of France. His plane disappeared over the water, and he was never seen again.

Over the decades since *The Little Prince* was published, it has gone on to become one of the best-selling novels of all time. In 2003, a small moon in our solar system's asteroid belt was named Petit-Prince in honor of the masterpiece Saint-Exupéry created.

Twenty-First Century

The Little Prince is a landmark of literature and one of the most translated and beloved books in the world. It tackles universal topics with a unique philosophical and poetic sensibility. Sixty-five years after the first edition, the Saint-Exupéry Estate decided to bring the character back for a whole new generation . . . and for everyone who has ever loved the boy who sees the world with his heart.

The Little Prince now returns in a series of new adventures that remain true to the spirit of the original work. He will travel from planet to planet chasing the wicked Snake, who wants to plunge the whole universe into darkness. On each planet, the Snake sends bad thoughts into the minds of its inhabitants, making them sad and grim, draining the life out of their planet. The Little Prince must leave his beautiful Rose behind and must use his vision and courage to defeat the Snake, bringing along his friend Fox to save planets in danger across the universe.

About the Adapters

After several years in video games and Japanese animation, adapter Guillaume Dorison became literary editor for the publisher Les Humanoïdes Associés in 2006, where he launched the Shogun Collection dedicated to original manga. In June 2010, he founded Élyum Studio with Didier Poli, Jean-Baptiste Hostache, and Xavier Dorison to provide services for the creation of graphic novels. In addition to his position as director of writing for Élyum Studio, he has more than two dozen comics and manga to his credit under the pseudonym IZU, has written several titles in the Explora series on world explorers for French publisher Glénat, and won the 2010 Animeland Prize for best French manga.

Didier Poli, artistic director for the new graphic novel adaptations based on The Little Prince, was born in Lyon in 1971. After graduate studies in applied arts, he worked for various animation studios including Disney. He was working as artistic director for the video game company Kalisto Entertainment when he met Manuel Bichebois in 2001 and began drawing Bichebois' graphic novel series L'Enfant de l'orage. At the 2004 Nîmes Festival, Didier Poli received the Bronze Boar prize for young talent. He continues, along with his work on graphic novels, to work regularly in cartoons and video games as a designer and storyboard artist.

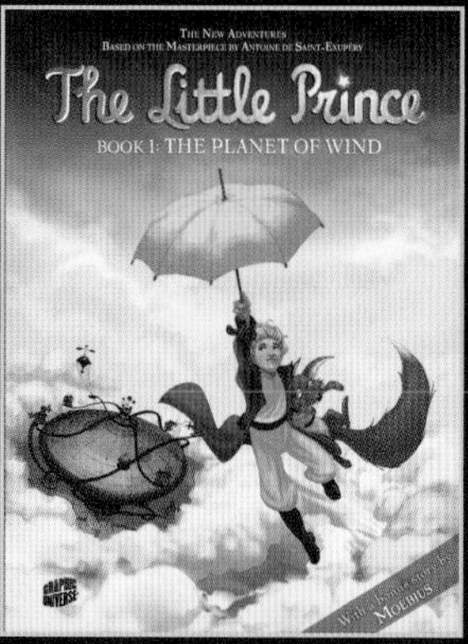
The New Adventures
Based on the Masterpiece by Antoine de Saint-Exupéry
The Little Prince
BOOK 1: THE PLANET OF WIND

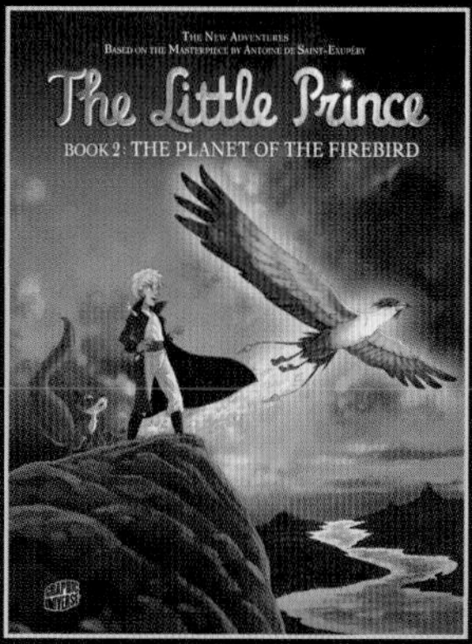
The New Adventures
Based on the Masterpiece by Antoine de Saint-Exupéry
The Little Prince
BOOK 2: THE PLANET OF THE FIREBIRD

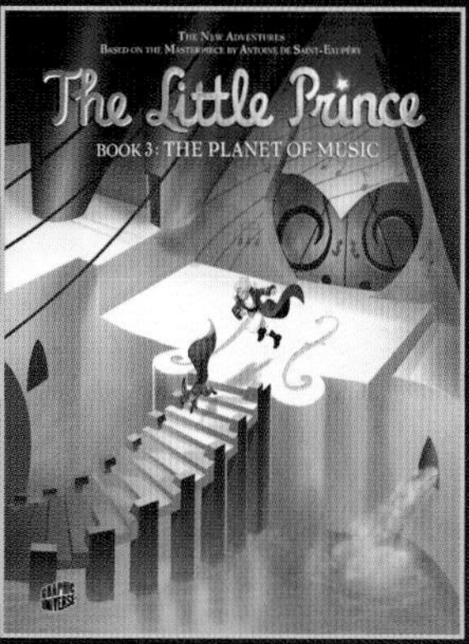
The New Adventures
Based on the Masterpiece by Antoine de Saint-Exupéry
The Little Prince
BOOK 3: THE PLANET OF MUSIC

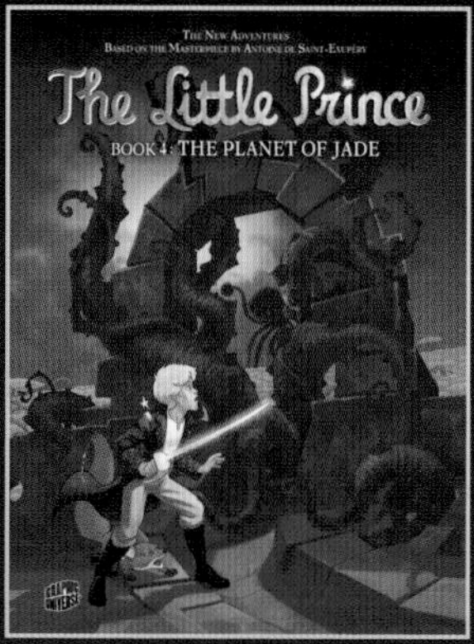
The New Adventures
Based on the Masterpiece by Antoine de Saint-Exupéry
The Little Prince
BOOK 4: THE PLANET OF JADE

BOOK 1: THE PLANET OF WIND

BOOK 2: THE PLANET OF THE FIREBIRD

BOOK 3: THE PLANET OF MUSIC

BOOK 4: THE PLANET OF JADE

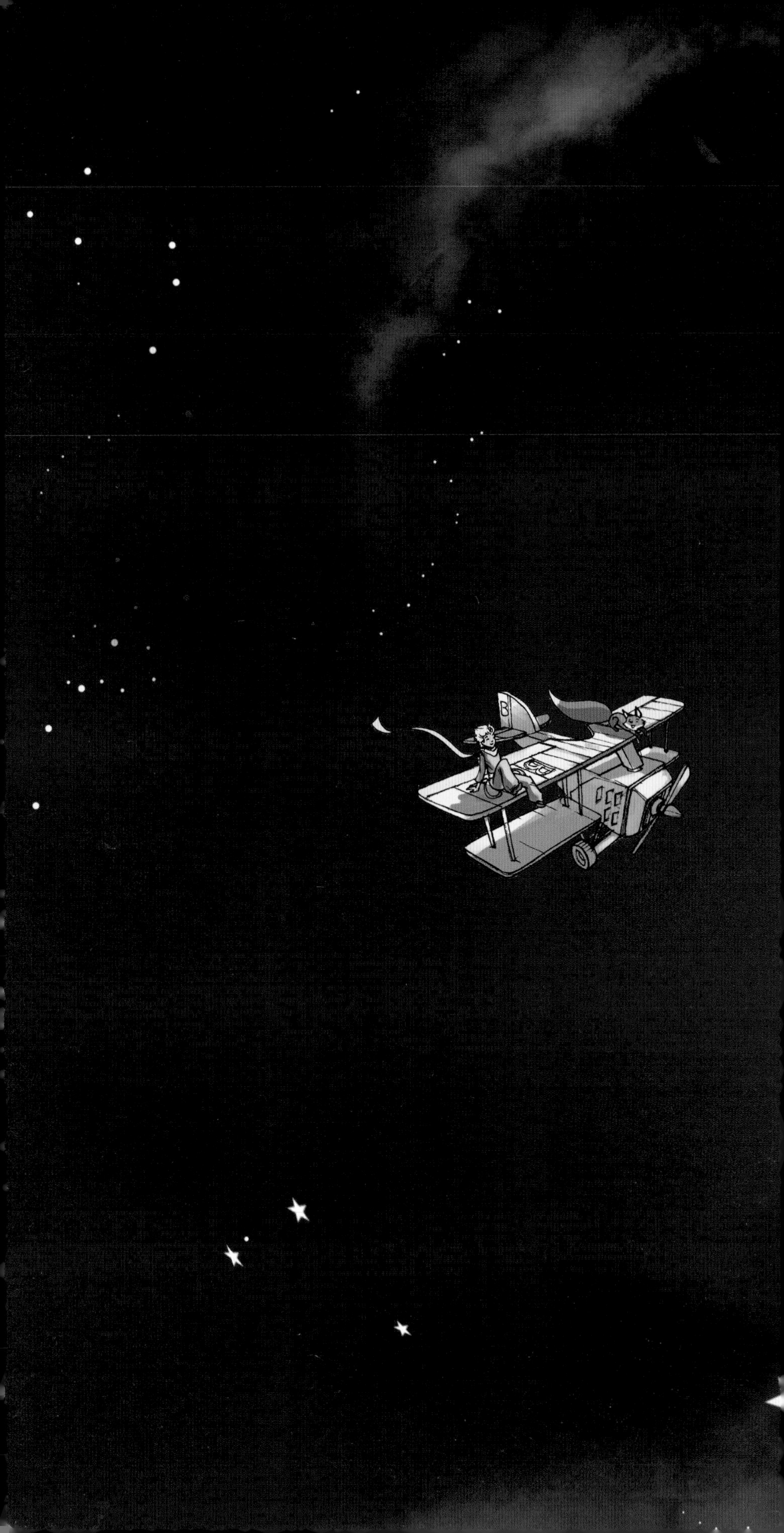

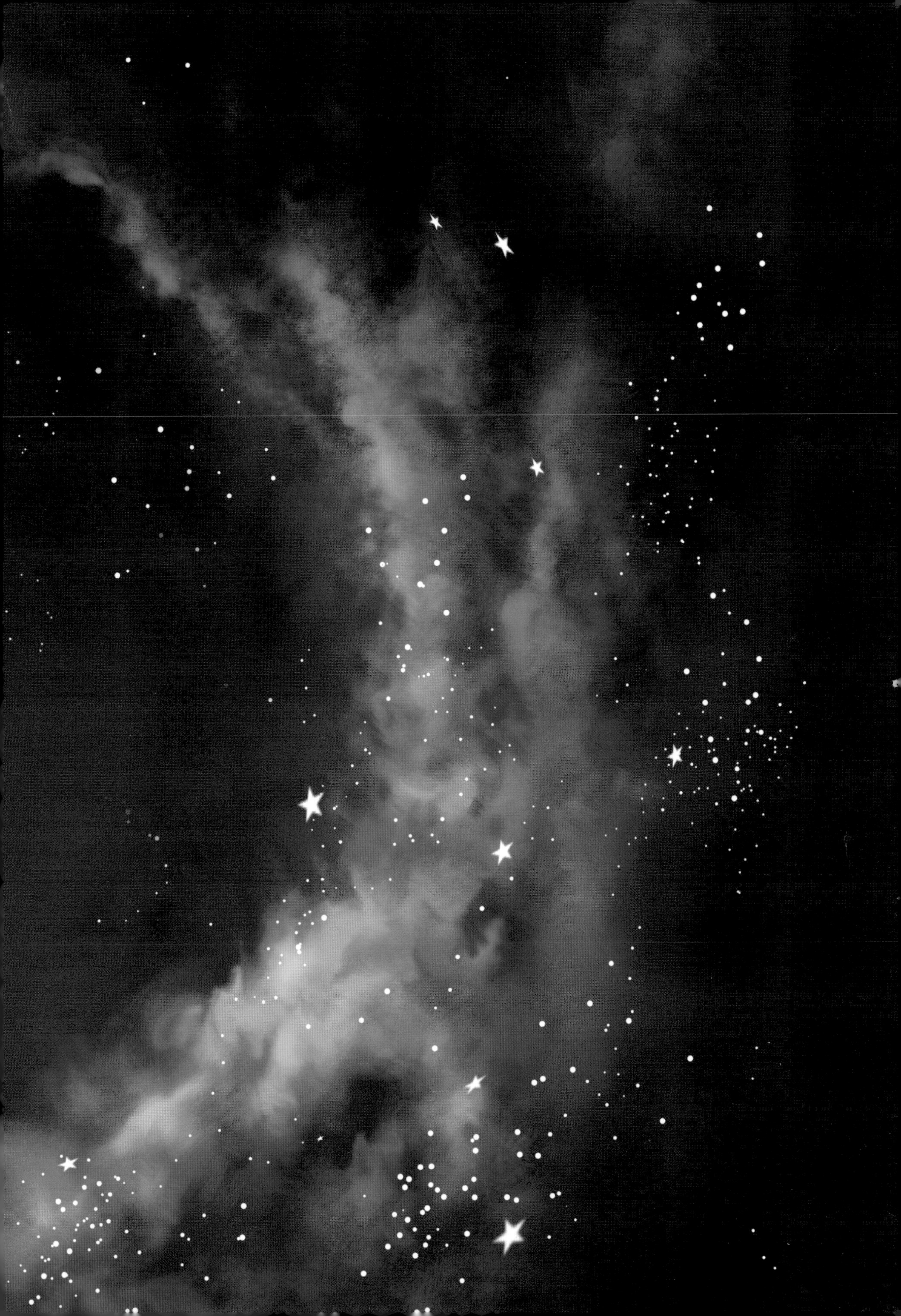